"Wallace was both satirist and preacher in the same breath, and the idea that the IRS, imagined as a quasi-religious foundation in which the burdensome and egotistic self might find redemption in the service of a greater good, could be both a comic conceit and a heartfelt belief seems to have been central to his conception of *The Pale King*."
—Jonathan Raban, *New York Review of Books*

"It's easy and seems obvious to say that Wallace the novelist was an ethicist, deeply concerned with fidelity to the truth. He didn't flinch from plumbing the scariest, strangest, most difficult things right to the bottom: scenes of psychic torture, or right-to-life Christians facing an unwanted pregnancy, of suicide or murder, addiction or philosophy, the mathematics of Georg Cantor or the ethics of eating meat. In fact, though, his fiction is full of whoppers. I mean plain lies, as in, you can't kill someone with ground glass (as in *The Pale King*) any more than you can use Lemon Pledge as sunscreen (as in *Infinite Jest*) . . . Why do this to us? It's to make us do the 'hard work,' as he used to call it, of reading well. Through these cascades of weird little fibs, reality itself is over and over called into question. All of it. Experience, reading, writing. *Being*."
—Maria Bustillos, *Popula*

"The risk Wallace takes is to guess that he is not the only 'obscenely well-educated,' curiously lost and empty white boy out there; that his sadness is also the experience of a whole historical moment . . . When I started reading Wallace, it was [his] directness that hit me hardest, this effort to speak openly and straightforwardly about things so obvious and so embarrassing that most of us, most of the time, just ignore them; this eager voice reaching out to touch its knuckles to my being, though both of us know there's nothing there, really, apart from printed words on a page."

—Jenny Turner, *London Review of Books*

"Wallace is famous for his ear for idiomatic expression, but he is often assumed to be merely listening rather than reconfiguring his generation's impoverished English at every turn . . . In fact Wallace takes our unremarkable, stammering colloquialisms and works them into monologues that are verbally and grammatically complex and highly literary, while also sounding like a real voice speaking to us. But it could only be the voice of one person, and it could only be written."

—Elaine Blair, *New York Review of Books*

"Imagine walking into a place, say a mega-chain copy shop in a strip mall. It's early morning, and you're the first customer. You stop under the bright fluorescents and let the doors glide closed behind you, look at the employees in their corporate-blue shirts, mouths open, shuffling around sleepily. You take them in as a unified image, with an impenetrable surface of vague boredom and dissatisfaction that you're content to be on the outside of, and you set to your task, to your copying or whatever. That's precisely the moment when Wallace hits pause, that first little turn into inattention, into self-absorption. He reverses back through it, presses play again. Now it's different. You're in a room with a bunch of human beings. Each of them, like you, is broken and has healed in some funny way. Each of them, even the shallowest, has a novel inside. Each is loved by God or deserves to be."

—John Jeremiah Sullivan, *GQ*

SOMETHING TO
DO WITH PAYING
ATTENTION

SOMETHING TO DO WITH PAYING ATTENTION

DAVID FOSTER WALLACE

WITH A FOREWORD BY SARAH McNALLY

McNally Editions

New York

McNally Editions
134 Prince St.
New York, NY 10012

ISBN: 978-1-946022-27-1
E-book: 978-1-946022-33-2

Designed by Jonathan D. Lippincott

5   7   9   10   8   6   4

FOREWORD

I first read David Foster Wallace as a young person in Winnipeg, Manitoba, a prairie city that is remote even by Canadian standards. Although *Infinite Jest* is (sort of) about a prep school in the northeastern United States, there was something about Wallace's voice—something democratic, Midwestern, unaffected, unabashedly interested and at home in the texture of everyday life—that felt familiar to me in a way that American voices rarely ever did. In fact, strange as it may seem, and despite obvious differences, the writer he reminded me of most was the great Ontarian Alice Munro. Wallace, like Munro, found me in my lived experience of language.

Wallace did a lot with his plainspoken English, like building a rocket ship out of stuff lying around the garage. *Infinite Jest* made me feel like a provincial kid who, for some reason, was granted a magical tutor, a Merlin or Mary Poppins–type figure, and shown a vastly more compelling world, in which my erstwhile concerns were refracted through the wise, humorous empathy of a greater mind.

In a pattern now familiar, and even expected, when you learn a lot about your favorite authors—including their mistakes, their limitations, their obsessions, their unheroic and problematic choices—they stop being wizards or magic nannies. You can't idealize them anymore. But sometimes idealization is replaced by admiration, exactly because your heroes were human, and because they transcended their flawed selves in their work. And when you stop idealizing them, you notice the writing more. What I notice now when I reread Wallace is the warmth underneath the brilliance.

Wallace, who made so many of my generation feel smarter than we ever had, who taught us it was OK and possibly necessary to do your thinking with a keyboard, on a screen, turned out to have been—also, and at the same time, and not coincidentally—awfully concerned with the state of our souls. And his famous "style," with its long sentences and footnotes, turned out to contain other modes, other styles. The footnotes weren't the important thing.

So it turned out, or so it turned out for me.

Something to Do with Paying Attention first appeared as part of *The Pale King*, the long, unfinished novel that Wallace left behind when he died in 2008. At one point, Wallace considered publishing "the novella" as a book of its own. In this sense, it is the last book he ever finished. (He never named it: the title is ours, not his.) Like the rest of *The Pale King*, it revolves around the IRS—specifically, an IRS Regional Examination Center, in Peoria, Illinois, circa 1985. The unnamed narrator turns up elsewhere as Chris Fogle (aka "Irrelevant Chris"); the interviewer turns out to be one "David Wallace," recently kicked out of college for selling term papers, now hired by the IRS for an internal research project.

None of this is necessary information, however. *Something to Do with Paying Attention* speaks for itself. It is, to my mind, not just a complete story, but the best complete example we have of Wallace's late style, where calm and poise replace the pyrotechnics of *Infinite Jest* and other early works. The characteristic irony is still there—in his own notes, Wallace refers to Chris as "an insufferable do-gooder"—but now the comedy is reflective, not frenetic. To borrow the language of the book, the storytelling is not just self-conscious, but self-aware, and aware of its very human failures. The narrator is an accountant, by vocation, who can't account for himself.

Something to Do with Paying Attention is something of an anomaly for McNally Editions, which is a reprint press: David Foster Wallace is hardly a forgotten author. If anything, his fame can get in the way of his work, and the vastness of his production can make it hard to find the unexpected gem. Yet for someone who has never read Wallace, I think this little book—funny, modest, afire with a gemlike flame—is a perfect place to start. And then, for those of us who grew up on Wallace, and partly *because* of Wallace, it is the perfect place to start again and read him with new eyes.

Sarah McNally
New York, 2021

SOMETHING TO
DO WITH PAYING
ATTENTION

I'm not sure I even know what to say. To be honest, a good bit of it I don't remember. I don't think my memory works in quite the way it used to. It may be that this kind of work changes you. Even just rote exams. It might actually change your brain. For the most part, it's now almost as if I'm trapped in the present. If I drank, for instance, some Tang, it wouldn't remind me of anything—I'd just taste the Tang.

From what I understand, I'm supposed to explain how I arrived at this career. Where I came from, so to speak, and what the Service means to me.

I think the truth is that I was the worst kind of nihilist—the kind who isn't even aware he's a nihilist. I was like a piece of paper on the street in the wind, thinking, 'Now I think I'll blow this way, now I think I'll blow that way.' My essential response to everything was 'Whatever.'

This was especially after high school, when I drifted for several years, in and out of three different colleges, one of them two different times, and four or five different majors. One of these might have been a minor. I was

pretty much of a wastoid. Essentially, I had no motivation, which my father referred to as 'initiative.' Also, I
remember that everything at that time was very fuzzy and
abstract. I took a lot of psychology and political science,
literature. Classes where everything was fuzzy and abstract
and open to interpretation and then those interpretations
were open to still more interpretations. I used to write my
class papers on the typewriter the day they were due, and
usually I got some type of B with 'Interesting in places' or
'Not too bad!' written underneath the grade as an instruc-
tional comment. The whole thing was just going through
the motions; it didn't mean anything—even the whole
point of the classes themselves was that nothing meant
anything, that everything was abstract and endlessly inter-
pretable. Except, of course, there was no argument about
the fact that you had to turn in the papers, you had to go
through the motions themselves, although nobody ever
explained just why, what your ultimate motivation was
supposed to be. I'm 99 percent sure that I took just one
Intro Accounting class during all this time, and did all
right in it until we hit depreciation schedules, as in the
straight-line method vs. accelerated depreciation, and the
combination of difficulty and sheer boredom of the depreciation schedules broke my initiative, especially after I'd
missed a couple of the classes and fallen behind, which
with depreciation is fatal—and I ended up dropping that
class and taking an incomplete. This was at Lindenhurst
College—the later Intro class at DePaul had the same title
but a somewhat different emphasis. I also remember that
incompletes peeved my father quite a bit more than a low
grade, understandably.

I know three separate times during this unmotivated period I withdrew from college and tried working so-called real jobs. One was that I was a security guard for a parking garage on North Michigan, or taking tickets for events at the Liberty Arena, or briefly on the production line at a Cheese Nabs plant working the cheese product injector, or working for a company which made and installed gymnasium floors. Then, after a while, I couldn't handle the boredom of the jobs, which were all unbelievably boring and meaningless, and I'd quit and enroll someplace else and essentially try to start college over again. My transcript looked like collage art. Understandably, this routine wore thin with my father, who was a cost systems supervisor for the City of Chicago—although during this time he lived in Libertyville, which is describable as an upper-bourgeois northern suburb. He used to say, dryly and with a perfectly straight face, that I was shaping up to be an outstanding twenty-yard-dash man. This was his way of squeezing my shoes. He read a great deal and was into dry, sardonic expressions. Although on one other occasion, after taking an incomplete or withdrawing somewhere and coming back home, I remember I was in the kitchen getting something to eat and heard him arguing with my mother and Joyce, telling them I couldn't find my ass with both hands. That was the angriest I think I ever saw him get during this unfocused period. I don't remember the exact context, but knowing how dignified and essentially reserved my father usually was, I'm sure I must have just done something especially feckless or pathetic to provoke him. I don't remember my mother's response or exactly how I came to overhear the remark, as eavesdropping on your parents seems like something that only a much smaller child would do.

My mother was more sympathetic, and whenever my father started squeezing my shoes about the lack-of-direction thing, my mother would stick up for me to some extent and say I was trying to find my path in life, and that not every path is outlined in neon lights like an airport runway, and that I owed it to myself to find my path and let things unfold in their own way. From what I understand of basic psychology, this is a fairly typical dynamic—son is feckless and lacks direction, mother is sympathetic and believes in son's potential and sticks up for him, father is peeved and endlessly criticizes and squeezes son's shoes but still, when push comes to shove, always ponies up the check for the next college. I can remember my father referring to money as 'that universal solvent of ambivalence' in connection with these tuition checks. I should mention that my mother and father were amicably divorced by this time, which was also somewhat typical of that era, so there were all those typical divorce dynamics in play as well, psychologically. The same sort of dynamics were probably being played out in homes all over America—the child trying to sort of passively rebel while still financially tied to the parent, and all the typical psychological business that goes along with that.

Anyhow, all this was in the Chicagoland area in the 1970s, a period that now seems as abstract and unfocused as I was myself. Maybe the Service and I have this in common—that the past decade seems much longer ago than it really was, because of what's happened in the intervening time. As for myself, I had trouble just paying attention, and the things I can remember now seem mostly pointless. I mean really remember, not just have a general impression of. I remember having fairly long hair, meaning long on all four sides, but nevertheless it was also always parted on the left side and held in place with spray from a dark red can. I remember the color of this can. I can't think of this period's hair without almost wincing. I can remember things I wore—a lot of burnt orange and brown, red-intensive paisley, bell-bottom cords, acetate and nylon, flared collars, dungaree vests. I had a metal peace-sign pendant that weighed half a pound. Docksiders and yellow Timberlands and a pair of shiny low brown leather dress boots which zipped up the sides and only the sharp toes showed under bell-bottoms. The little sensitive leather thong around the neck. The commercial psychedelia. The obligatory buckskin jacket. The dungarees whose cuffs dragged on the ground and dissolved into white thread. Wide belts, tube socks, track shoes from Japan. The standard getup. I remember the round, puffy winter coats of nylon and down that made us all look like parade balloons. The scratchy white painter's pants with loops for supposed tools down the side of the thigh. I remember everyone despising Gerald Ford, not so much for pardoning Nixon but for constantly falling down. Everyone had contempt for him. Very blue designer jeans. I remember the feminist tennis player Billie Jean King beating what seemed like an old and feeble man player on television and my mother and her friends all being very excited by this. 'Male chauvinist pig,' 'women's lib,' and 'stagflation' all seemed vague and indistinct to me during this time, like listening to background noise with half an ear. I don't remember what I did with all my real attention, what-all it was going towards. I never did anything, but at the same time I could normally never sit still and become aware of what was really going on. It's hard to explain. I somewhat remember a younger Cronkite, Barbara Walters, and Harry Reasoner—I don't think I watched much news. Again, I suspect this was more typical than I thought at the time. One thing you learn in Rote Exams is how disorganized and inattentive most people are and how little they pay attention to what's going on outside of their sphere. Somebody named Howard K. Smith was also big in news, I remember. You almost never hear the word *ghetto* anymore, now. I remember Acapulco Gold versus Colombia Gold, Ritalin versus Ritadex, Cylert and Obetrol, Laverne and Shirley, Carnation Instant Breakfast, John Travolta, disco fever, and children's tee shirts with the 'Fonz' on them. And 'Keep On Truckin'' shirts, which my mother loved, where walking people's shoes and soles looked abnormally large. Actually preferring, like most children my age, Tang to real orange juice. Mark Spitz and Johnny Carson, the celebration in 1976 with fleets of antique ships coming into a harbor on TV. Smoking pot after school in high school and then watching TV and eating Tang out of the jar with a finger, wetting my finger and sticking it in, over and over, until I'd look down and couldn't believe how much of the jar was gone. Sitting there with my wastoid friends, and so on and so forth—and none of it meant anything. It's like I was dead or asleep without even being aware of it, as in the Wisconsin expression 'didn't know enough to lay down.'

I remember in high school getting Dexedrine from a kid whose mother had them prescribed for her for pep, and the weird way they tasted, and the remarkable way they made the thing of counting while reading or speaking disappear—they were called black beauties—but the way after a while they made your lower back ache and gave you terrible, terrible breath. Your mouth tasted like a long-dead frog in a cloudy jar in Biology when you first opened the jar. It's still sickening just to think about. There was also the period when my mother was so upset when Richard Nixon got reelected so easily, which I remember because it was around then that I tried Ritalin, which I bought from a guy in World Cultures class whose little brother in primary school was supposedly on Ritalin from a doctor who didn't keep track of his prescriptions very well, and which some people didn't think were anything special compared to black beauties, Ritalin, but I liked them very much, at first because it made sitting and studying for long periods of time possible and even interesting, and which I really, really liked, but it was hard to get much of—Ritalin was— especially after evidently the little brother wigged out one day at primary school from not taking his Ritalin and the parents and doctor discovered the irregularities with the prescriptions and suddenly there was no pimply guy in pink sunglasses selling four-dollar Ritalin pills out of his locker in junior hall.

I seem to remember in 1976 my father openly predict- ing a Ronald Reagan presidency and even sending their campaign a donation—although in retrospect I don't think Reagan even really ran in '76. This was my life before the sudden change in direction and eventually entering the Service. Girls wore caps or dungaree hats, but most guys were essentially uncool if they wore a hat. Hats were things to make fun of. Baseball caps were for the rednecks downstate. Older men of any seriousness still sometimes wore business-type hats outside, though. I can remember my father's hat now almost better than his face under it. I used to spend time imagining what my father's face looked like when he was alone—I mean his facial expression and eyes—when he was by himself in his office at work at the City Hall annex downtown and there was no one to shape a certain expression for. I remember my father wearing madras shorts on weekends, and black socks, and mowing the lawn like that, and sometimes looking out of the window at what he looked like in that getup and feeling actual pain at being related to him. I remember everyone pretending to be a samurai or saying, 'Excuse *me!*' in all sorts of different contexts—this was cool. To show approval or excitement, we said, 'Excellent.' In college, you could hear the word *excellent* five thousand times a day. I remember some of my attempts to grow sideburns at DePaul and always ending up shaving them off, because at a certain point they got to where they looked just like pubic hair. The smell of Brylcreem in my father's hatband, Deep Throat, Howard Cosell, my mother's throat showing ligaments on either side when she and Joyce laughed. Throwing her hands around or bending over. Mom was always a very physical laugher—her whole body gets involved.

There was also the word *mellow* that was used constantly, although even early on in its use this word bugged me; I just didn't like it. I still probably used it sometimes, though, without being aware I was doing it.

My mother's the sort of somewhat lanky type of older woman who seems to become almost skinny and tough with age instead of ballooning out, becoming ropy and sharp-jointed and her cheekbones even more pronounced. I remember sometimes thinking of beef jerky when I would first see her, and then feeling terrible that I had that association. She was quite good-looking in her day, though, and some of the later weight-loss was also nerve-related, because after the thing with my father her nerves got worse and worse. Admittedly, too, one other factor in her sticking up for me with my father as to drifting in and out of school was the past trouble I'd had with reading in primary school when we'd lived in Rockford and my father had worked for the City of Rockford. This was in the mid-1960s, at Machesney Elementary. I went through a sudden period where I couldn't read. I mean that I actually could read—my mother knew I could read from when we'd read children's books together. But for almost two years at Machesney, instead of reading something I'd count the words in it, as though reading was the same as just counting the words. For example, 'Here came Old Yeller, to save me from the hogs' would equate to ten words which I would count off from one to ten instead of its being a sentence that made you love Old Yeller in the book even more. It was a strange problem in my developmental wiring at the time which caused a lot of trouble and embarrassment and was one reason why we ended up moving to the Chicagoland area, because for a while it looked as though I would have to attend a special school in Lake Forest. I have very little memory of this time except for the feeling of not especially wanting to count words or intending to but just not being able to help it—it was frustrating and strange. It got worse under pressure or nervousness, which is typical of things like that. Anyhow, part of my mother's fierce defense of letting me experience and learn things in my own way dates from that time, when the Rockford School District reacted to the reading problem in all sorts of ways that she didn't think were helpful or fair. Some of her consciousness-raising and entry into the women's lib movement of the 1970s probably also dates from that time of fighting the bureaucracy of the school district. I still sometimes lapse into counting words, or rather usually the counting goes on when I'm reading or talking, as a sort of background noise or unconscious process, a little like breathing.

For instance, I've said 2,752 words right now since I started. Meaning 2,752 words as of just before I said, 'I've said,' versus 2,754 if you count 'I've said'—which I do, still. I count numbers as one word no matter how large a given number is. Not that it actually means anything—it's more like a mental tic. I don't remember exactly when it started. I know I had no trouble learning to read or reading the Sam and Ann books they teach you to read with, so it must have been after second grade. I know that my mother, as a child in Beloit, WI, where she grew up, had an aunt who had a thing of washing her hands over and over without being able to stop, which eventually got so bad she had to go to a rest home. I seem to remember thinking of my mother as in some way associating the counting thing more with that aunt at the sink and not seeing it as a form of retardation or inability to just sit there and read as instructed, which is how Rockford school authorities seemed to see it. Anyhow, hence her hatred of traditional institutions and authority, which was another thing that helped gradually alienate her from my father and imperil their marriage, and so on and so forth.

I remember once, in I think 1975 or '76, shaving off just one sideburn and going around like that for a period of time, believing the one sideburn made me a nonconformist— I'm not kidding—and getting into long, serious conversations with girls at parties who would ask me what the lone sideburn 'meant.' A lot of the things I remember saying and believing during this period make me literally wince now, to think of it. I remember KISS, REO Speedwagon, Cheap Trick, Styx, Jethro Tull, Rush, Deep Purple, and, of course, good old Pink Floyd. I remember BASIC and COBOL. COBOL was what my father's cost systems hardware ran at his office. He was incredibly knowledgeable about the era's computers. I remember Sony's wide pocket transistors and the way that many of the city's blacks held their radios up to their ear whereas white kids from the suburbs used the optional little earplug, like a CID earbud, which had to be cleaned almost daily or else it got really foul. There was the energy crisis and recession and stagflation, though I cannot remember the order in which these occurred—although I do know the main energy crisis must have happened when I was living back at home after the Lindenhurst College thing, because I got my mother's tank siphoned out while out partying late at night with old high school friends, which my father was not thrilled about, understandably. I think New York City actually went bankrupt for a while during this period. There was also the 1977 disaster of the State of Illinois's experiment with making the state sales tax a progressive tax, which I know upset my father a lot but which I neither understood nor cared about at the time. Later, of course, I would understand why making a sales tax progressive is such a terrible idea, and why the resulting chaos more or less cost the governor at the time his job. At the time, though, I don't remember noticing anything except the unusually terrible crowds and hassle of shopping for the holidays in late '77. I don't know if that's relevant. I doubt anyone outside the state cares very much about this, though there are still some jokes about it among the older wigglers at the REC.

I remember feeling the actual physical feeling of hatred of most commercial rock—such as for disco, which if you were cool you pretty much had to hate, and all rock groups with one-word place names. Boston, Kansas, Chicago, America—I can still feel an almost bodily hatred. And believing that I and maybe one or two friends were among the very, very few people who truly understood what Pink Floyd was trying to say. It's embarrassing. Most of these almost feel like some other person's memories. I remember almost none of early childhood, mostly just weird little isolated strobes. The more fragmented the memory is, though, the more it seems to feel authentically mine, which is strange. I wonder if anyone feels as though they're the same person they seem to remember. It would probably make them have a nervous breakdown. It probably wouldn't even make any sense.

I don't know if this is enough. I don't know what anybody else has told you.

Our common word for this kind of nihilist at the time was *wastoid*.

I remember rooming in a high-rise UIC dorm with a very mod, with-it sophomore from Naperville who also wore sideburns and a leather thong and played the guitar. He saw himself as a nonconformist, and also very unfocused and nihilistic, and deeply into the school's wastoid drug scene, and drove what I have to admit was a very cool-looking 1972 Firebird that it eventually turned out his parents paid the insurance on. I cannot remember his name, try as I might. UIC stood for the University of Illinois, Chicago Campus, a gigantic urban university. The dorm we roomed in was right on Roosevelt, and our main windows faced a large downtown podiatric clinic—I can't remember its name, either—which had a huge raised electrified neon sign that rotated on its pole every weekday from 8:00 to 8:00 with the name and mnemonic phone number ending in 3668 on one side and on the other a huge colored outline of a human foot—our best guess was a female foot, from the proportions—and I remember that this roommate and I formulated a kind of ritual in which we'd make sure to try to be at the right spot at our windows at 8:00 each night to watch the foot sign go dark and stop rotating when the clinic closed. It always went dark at the same time the clinic's windows did and we theorized that everything was on one main breaker. The sign's rotation didn't stop all at once. It more like slowly wound down, with almost a wheel-of-fortune quality about where it would finally stop. The ritual was that if the sign stopped with the foot facing away, we would go to the UIC library and study, but if it stopped with the foot or any significant part of it facing our windows, we would take it as a 'sign' (with the incredibly obvious

double entendre) and immediately blow off any homework or supposed responsibility we had and go instead
to the Hat, which at that time was the currently hip UIC
pub and place to hear bands, and would drink beers and
play quarters and tell all the other kids whose parents
were paying their tuition about the ritual of the rotating
foot in a way that we all appeared nihilistically wastoid
and hip. I'm seriously embarrassed to remember things
like this. I can remember the podiatrist's sign and the
Hat and what the Hat looked and even smelled like, but
I cannot remember this roommate's name, even though
we probably hung out together three or four nights a week
that year. The Hat had no relation to Meibeyer's, which is
the main sort of pub for rote examiners here at the REC,
and also has a hat motif and an elaborate display-rack of
hats, but these are meant to be historical IRS and CPA
hats, the hats of serious adults. Meaning the similarity is
just a coincidence. There were actually two Hats, as in a
franchise—there was the UIC one on Cermak and Western, and another one down in Hyde Park for the more
motivated, focused kids at U of Chicago. Everybody at
our Hat called the Hyde Park Hat 'the Yarmulke.' This
roommate was not a bad or evil guy, although he turned
out to be able to play only three or four real songs on the
guitar, which he played over and over and over, and bla-
tantly rationalized his selling of drugs as a form of social
rebellion instead of just pure capitalism, and even at the
time I knew he was a total conformist to the late-seventies
standards of so-called nonconformity, and sometimes I
felt contemptuous of him. I might have despised him
a little. As if I was exempt, of course—but this kind

of blatant projection and displacement was part of the nihilist hypocrisy of the whole period.

I can remember the 'Uncola,' and the way Noxzema commercials always played a big bump-and-grind theme. I seem to remember a lot of wood-pattern designs on things that were not wood, and station wagons with side panels engineered to look like wood. I remember Jimmy Carter addressing the nation in a cardigan, and something about Carter's brother turning out to be a wastoid and public boob embarrassing the president just by being related to him.

I don't think I voted. The truth is that I don't remember if I voted or not. I probably planned to and said I was going to and then got distracted somehow and didn't get around to it. That would be about par for the period.

Obviously, it probably goes without saying that I partied heavily during this whole period. I don't know how much I should say about this. But I didn't party any more or less than everyone else I knew did—in fact, very precisely neither more nor less. Everyone I knew and hung out with was a wastoid, and we knew it. It was hip to be ashamed of it, in a strange way. A weird kind of narcissistic despair. Or just to feel directionless and lost—we romanticized it. I did like Ritalin and certain types of speed like Cylert, which was a little unusual, but everyone had their idiosyncratic favorites when it came to partying. I didn't do incredible amounts of speed, as the kinds I liked were hard to get—you more had to stumble across it. The roommate with the blue Firebird was obsessed with hashish, which he always described as *mellow.*

Looking back, I doubt if it ever occurred to me that the way I felt towards this roommate was probably the way my father felt about me—that I was just as much a conformist as he was, plus a hypocrite, a 'rebel' who really just sponged off of society in the form of his parents. I wish I could say I was aware enough for this contradiction to sink in at the time, although I probably would have just turned it into some kind of hip, nihilistic joke. At the same time, sometimes I know I worried about my directionlessness and lack of initiative, how abstract and open to different interpretations everything seemed at the time, even about how fuzzy and pointless my memories were starting to seem. My father, on the other hand, I know, remembered everything—in particular, physical details, the precise day and time of appointments, and past statements which were now inconsistent with present statements. But then, I would learn that this sort of close attention and total recall was part of his job.

What I really was was naive. For instance, I knew I lied, but I hardly ever assumed that anybody else around me might be lying. I realize now how conceited that is, and how unfocused that lets actual reality be. I was a child, really. The truth is that most of what I really know about myself I learned in the Service. That may sound too much like sucking up, but it's the truth. I've been here five years, and I've learned an incredible amount.

Anyhow, I can also recall smoking pot with my mother and her partner, Joyce. They grew their own, and it wasn't exactly potent, but that wasn't really the point, because with them it was more of a sort of liberated political state-ment than a matter of getting high, and my mother almost seemed to make it a point to smoke pot whenever I was over there visiting them, and while it made me a little uncomfortable, I don't ever remember refusing to 'fire up' with them, even though it embarrassed me somewhat when they used college terms like this. At that time, my mother and Joyce co-owned a small feminist bookstore, which I knew my father resented having helped finance through the divorce settlement. And I can remember once sitting around on their Wrigleyville apartment's beanbag chairs, passing around one of their large, amateurishly rolled doobersteins—which was the hip, wastoid term for a joint at that time, at least around the Chicagoland area—and listening to my mother and Joyce recount very vivid, detailed memories from their early childhoods, and both of them laughing and crying and stroking one another's hair in emotional support, which didn't really bother me—their touching or even kissing one another in front of me—or at least by then I'd had plenty of time to get used to it, but I can remember becoming more and more paranoid and nervous at the time, because, when I tried hard to think of some of my own childhood memories, the only really vivid memory I could remember involved me pounding Glovolium into my Rawlings catcher's mitt, which my father had gotten me, and that day of getting the Johnny Bench Autograph mitt I remembered very well, although Mom and Joyce's was not the place to wax all sentimental about my father getting me something, obviously. The worst part was then starting to hear my mother recount all these memories and anecdotes of my own childhood, and realizing that she actually remembered much more of my early childhood than I did, as though somehow she'd seized or confiscated memories and experiences that were technically mine. Obviously, I didn't think of the term *seize* at the time. That's more a Service term. But smoking pot with my mother and Joyce was usually just not a pleasant experience at all, and often totally weirded me out, now that I think about it—and yet I did it with them almost every time. I doubt my mother enjoyed it much, either. The whole thing had an air of pretense of fun and liberation about it. In retrospect, I get the feeling that my mom was trying to get me to see her as changing and growing up right there with me, both on my side of the generation gap, as though we were still as close as we were when I was a child. As both being nonconformists and giving my father the finger, symbolically. Anyhow, smoking pot with her and Joyce always felt a bit hypocritical. My parents split up in February 1972, in the same week that Edmund Muskie cried in public on the campaign trail, and the TV had clips of him crying over and over. I can't remember what he was crying about, but it definitely sunk his chances in the campaign. It was the sixth week of theater class in high school where I first learned the term *nihilist*. I know I didn't feel any real hostility towards Joyce, by the way, although I do remember always feeling sort of edgy when it was just her and me, and being relieved when my mother got home and I could sort of relate to both of them as a couple instead of trying to make conversation with Joyce, which was always complicated because there always felt like a great deal more subjects and things to remember not to bring up than there were to actually talk about, so that trying to make chitchat with her was like trying to slalom at Devil's Head if the slalom's gates were only inches apart.

In hindsight, I realized later that my father was actually kind of witty and sophisticated. At the time, I think I

thought of him as barely alive, as like a robot or slave to
conformity. It's true that he was uptight, anal, and quick
with the put-downs. He was a hundred percent conventional establishment, and totally on the other side of the
generation gap—he was forty-nine when he died, which
was in December 1977, which obviously means he grew up
during the Depression. But I don't think I ever appreciated
his sense of humor about all of it—there was a way he sort
of wove his pro-establishment views into a dry, witty style
that I don't remember ever getting or understanding his
jokes in at the time. I didn't have much of a sense of humor
then, it seems, or else I did the standard child's thing of
taking everything he said as a personal comment or judgment. There was stuff I knew about him, which I'd picked
up through the years of childhood, mostly from my
mother. Like that he'd been really, really shy when they'd
first met. How he had wanted to go to more than just
technical college but he had bills to pay—he was in logistics and supply in Korea but had already gotten married to
my mother before he was posted overseas, and so upon
discharge he immediately had to find a job. This is what
people her age did then, she explained—if you met the
right person and were at least out of high school, you got
married, without even ever really thinking about it or questioning yourself. The point is that he was very smart and
somewhat unfulfilled, like many of his generation. He
worked hard because he had to, and his own dreams were
put on the back burner. This is all indirectly, from my
mother, but it fit with certain bits and pieces that even I
couldn't help being aware of. For instance, my father read
all the time. He was constantly reading. It was his whole

recreation, especially after the divorce—he was always coming home from the library with a stack of books with that clear library plastic wrap on the covers. I never paid any attention to what the books were or why he read so much—he never talked about what he was reading. I don't even know what his favorite kinds were, as in history, mysteries, or what. Looking back now, I think he was lonely, especially after the divorce, as the only people you could call his friends were colleagues from his job, and I think he essentially found his job boring—I don't think he felt much personal investment in the City of Chicago's budget and expenditure protocols, especially as it wasn't his idea to move here—and I think books and intellectual issues were one of his escapes from boredom. He was actually a very smart person. I wish I could remember more examples of the sort of things he'd say—at the time, I think they seemed more hostile or judgmental than like he was making fun of both of us at the same time. I do remember he sometimes referred to the so-called younger generation (meaning mine) as 'This thing America hath wrought.' That's not a very good example. It's almost like he thought the blame went both ways, that there was something wrong with the whole country's adults if they could produce kids like this in the 1970s. I remember once in October or November 1976, at twenty-one, during another period of time off, after being enrolled at DePaul—which actually didn't go well at all, the first time I was at DePaul. It was basically a disaster. They kind of invited me to leave, actually, which was the only time that had happened. The other times, at Lindenhurst College and then later at UIC, I'd withdrawn on my own. Anyhow, during this time off, I was working the second shift at a Cheese Nabs factory in Buffalo Grove and living there at my father's house in Libertyville. There was no way I was crashing at my mother and Joyce's apartment in the Wrigleyville section of Chicago, where the rooms all had bead curtains instead of doors. But I didn't have to punch in at this mindless job until six, so I'd mostly just hang around the house all afternoon until it was time to leave. And sometimes during this period my father would be away for a couple of days—like the Service, the City of Chicago's financial departments were always sending their more technical people to conferences and in-services, which I would come to learn later here in the Service are not like the big drunken conventions of private industry but are usually highly intensive and work-centered. My father said the city in-services were mostly just tedious, which was a word he used a fair amount, *tedious*. And on these trips it was just me living in the house, and you can imagine what used to happen when I'd be there on my own, especially on weekends, even though I was supposed to be in charge of looking after the house while he was gone. But the memory is of him coming home early one afternoon in '76 from one of these work trips, like a day or two before I'd thought he told me he was going to be home, and coming in the front door and finding me and two of my old so-called friends from Libertyville South high school in the living room—which, due to the slightly raised design of the front porch and front door, was in effect a sunken living room that more or less started right inside the front door, with one small set of stairs leading down into the living room and another set leading up to the house's second floor. Architecturally, the house's style is known as a raised ranch, like most of the other older homes on the street, and it had another set of stairs leading from the second-floor hallway down into the garage, which actually supports part of the second story—that is, the garage is, structurally, a necessary part of the house, which is what's distinctive about a raised ranch. At the moment he entered, two of us were slumped on the davenport with our dirty feet up on his special coffee table, and the carpeting was all littered with beer cans and Taco Bell wrappers—the cans were my father's beer, which he bought in bulk twice a year and stored in the utility room closet and normally drank maybe a total of two per week of—with us sitting there totally wasted and watching *The Searchers* on WGN, and one of the guys listening to Deep Purple on my father's special stereo head-phones for listening to classical music on, and the coffee table's special oak or maple top with big rings of conden-sation from the beer cans all over it because we'd turned the house's heat way up past where he normally allowed it to be, in terms of energy conservation and expense, and the other guy next to me on the davenport leaning over in the middle of taking a huge bong hit—this guy was famous for being able to take massive hits. Plus, the whole living room reeked. When then, suddenly, in the memory, I heard the distinctive sound of his footsteps on the broad wooden porch and the sound of his key in the front door, and only a second later my father suddenly comes in on a wave of very cold, clear air through the doorway with his hat and overnight bag—I was in the paralyzed shock of the totally busted kid, and I sat there paralyzed, unable to do any-thing and yet seeing each frame of him coming in with horrible focus and clarity—and him standing there at the edge of the few stairs down to the living room, taking his hat off with the trademark gesture that involved both his head and his hand as he stood there taking in the scene and the three of us—he'd made no secret of not much liking these old high school friends, who were the same guys I'd been out partying with when my mom's gas cap was stolen and the tank siphoned out, and none of us had any money left by the time we found the car, and I had to call my father and he had to take the train down after work to pay for gas so I could get the Le Car back to my mom and Joyce, who co-owned it and used it for bookstore business—with the three of us now slumped there all totally wasted and paralyzed, one of the guys wearing a ratty old tee shirt that actually said FUCK YOU across the chest, the other coughing out his mammoth hit in shock, so that a plume of pot smoke went rolling out across the living room towards my father—in short, my memory is of the scene being the worst confirmation of the worst kind of generation-gap stereotype and parental disgust for their decadent, wastoid kids, and of my father slowly putting down his bag and case and just standing there, with no expression and not saying anything for what felt like such a long time, and then he slowly made a gesture of putting one arm up in the air a little and looking up and said, '*Look on my works, ye mighty, and despair!*,' and then picked up his overnight bag again and without a word walked up the upstairs stairs and went into their old bedroom and closed the door. He didn't slam it, but you could hear the door close quite firmly. The memory, strangely, which is horribly sharp and detailed up to there, then totally stops, like a tape that's just run out, and I don't know what happened after that, like getting the guys out of there and hurriedly trying to clean everything up and turn the thermostat back down to sixty-eight, though I do remember feeling like complete shit, not so much like I'd been 'busted' or was in trouble as just childish, like a spoiled little selfish child, and imagining what I must have looked like to him, sitting there in litter in his house, wasted, with my dirty feet on the marked-up coffee table he and my mother had saved up for and gotten at an antique store in Rockford when they were still young and didn't have much money, and which he prized, and rubbed lemon oil in all the time, and said all he asked was that I should please keep my feet off of it and use a coaster—like, for a second or two seeing what I actually must have looked like to him as he stood there looking at us treating his living room like that. It wasn't a pretty picture, and it felt even worse as he hadn't yelled or squeezed my shoes about it—he just looked weary, and sort of embarrassed for both of us—and I remember for a second or two I could actually feel what he must have been feeling, and for an instant saw myself through his eyes, which made the whole thing much, much worse than if he'd been furious, or yelled, which he never did, not even the next time he and I were alone in the same room— which I don't remember when this was, like whether I skulked out of the house after cleaning everything up or whether I stayed there to face him. I don't know which one I did. I didn't even understand what he said, although obviously I understood he was being sarcastic, and in some way blaming himself or making fun of himself for having produced the 'work' that had just thrown the Taco Bell wrappers and bags on the floor instead of bothering to get up and take like eight steps to throw them away. Although later on, I just stumbled on the poem it turned out he was quoting from, in some kind of weird context at the Indianapolis TAC, and my eyes just about bulged out of my head, because I hadn't even known it was a poem—and a famous one, by the same British poet who evidently wrote the original *Frankenstein*. And I didn't even know my father read British poetry, much less that he could quote from it when he was upset. In short, there was probably much more to him than I was aware of, and I don't remember even realizing how little I knew about him, really, until after he was gone and it was too late. I expect that this sort of regret is typical, as well.

Anyhow, this one terrible memory of looking up from the davenport and seeing myself through his eyes, and of his sad, sophisticated way of expressing how sad and disgusted he was—this kind of sums up the whole period for me now, when I think of it. I also remember both of those former friends' names, too, from that fucked-up day, but obviously that's not relevant.

Things began to get much more vivid, focused, and concrete in 1978, and in retrospect I suppose I agree with Mom and Joyce that this was the year I 'found myself' or 'put away childish things' and began the process of developing some initiative and direction in my life, which obviously led to my joining the Service.

Though it's not directly connected to my choice of the IRS as a career, it's true that my father being killed in a public-transit accident in late 1977 was a sudden, horrible, and life-changing kind of event, which I obviously hope never to have to repeat in any way again. My mother took it especially hard, and had to go on tranquilizers, and she ended up being psychologically unable to sell my father's house, and left Joyce and the bookstore and moved back into the house in Libertyville, where she still lives today, with certain pictures of my father and of them as a young couple still in the house. It's a sad situation, and an armchair psychologist would probably say that she blamed herself somehow for the accident, even though I, more than anyone, would be in a position to know that that wasn't true, and that, in the final analysis, the accident was no one's fault. I was there when it happened—the accident—and there is no denying that it was one hundred percent terrible. Even today, I can remember the whole thing in such vivid, concrete detail that it almost seems more like a recording than a memory, which I'm told is not unusual for traumatic events—and yet there was also no way to recount for my mother exactly what happened from start to finish without almost destroying her, as she was already so grief-stricken, although just about anyone could have seen that a lot of her grief was unresolved conflicts and hang-ups over their marriage and the identity crisis she'd had in 1972 at age forty or forty-one and the divorce, none of which she got to really deal with at the time because she'd thrown herself so deeply into the women's lib movement and consciousness-raising and her new circle of strange, mostly overweight women who were all in their forties, plus her new sexual identity with Joyce almost right away, which I know must have just about killed my father, given how straitlaced and conventional he tended to be, although he and I never talked about it directly, and he and my mother somehow managed to stay reasonably good friends, and I never heard him say anything about the matter except some occasional bitching about how much of his agreed-upon support payments to her were going into the bookstore, which he sometimes referred to as 'that financial vortex' or just 'the vortex'—all of which is a whole long story in itself. So we never really talked about it, which I doubt is all that unusual in these sorts of cases.

If I had to describe my father, I would first say that my mother and father's marriage was one of the only ones I've seen in which the wife was noticeably taller than the man. My father was 5' 6" or 5' 6½", and not fat but stocky, the way many shorter men in their late forties are stocky. He might have weighed 170. He looked good in a suit—like so many men of his generation, his body almost seemed designed to fill out and support a suit. And he owned some good ones, most single-button and single-vent, understated and conservative, in mainly three-season worsteds and one or two seersucker for hot weather, in which he also eschewed his usual business hat. To his credit—at least in retrospect—he rejected the so-called modern style's wide ties, brighter colors, and flared lapels, and found the phenomenon of leisure suits or corduroy sport coats nauseating. His suits were not tailored, but they were nearly all from Jack Fagman, a very old and respected men's store in Winnetka which he had patronized ever since our family relocated to the Chicagoland area in 1964, and some of them were really nice. At home, in what he called his 'mufti,' he wore more casual slacks and double-knit dress shirts, sometimes under a sweater vest—his favorite of these was argyle. Sometimes he wore a cardigan, though

I think that he knew that cardigans made him look a little too broad across the beam. In the summer, there was sometimes the terrible thing of the Bermuda shorts with black dress socks, which it turned out were the only kind of socks my father even owned. One sport coat, a 36R in midnight-blue slubbed silk, had dated from his youth and early courtship of my mother, she had explained—it was hard for her to even hear about this jacket after the accident, much less help tell me what to do with it. The clothes closet contained his best and third-best topcoats, also from Jack Fagman, with the empty wooden hanger still between them. He used shoe trees for his dress and office footwear; some of these were inherited from his own father. ('These' obviously referring to the shoe trees, not the shoes.) There was also a pair of leather sandals which he'd received as a Christmas gift, and not only had never worn but hadn't even removed the catalogue tag from when it fell to me to go through his clothes closet and empty out the contents. The idea of lifts in his shoes would just never have occurred to my father. At that time, I had never to my knowledge seen a shoe tree, and didn't know what they were for, since I never took care of any of my shoes, or valued them.

My father's hair, which had evidently been almost light brown or blond when he was younger, had first darkened and then become suffused with gray, its texture stiffer than my own and tending to curl in the back during humid weather. The back of his neck was always red; his overall complexion was florid in the way that certain stocky older men's faces are florid or ruddy. Some of the redness was congenital, probably, and some psychological—like most men of his generation, he was both high-strung and tightly controlled, a type A personality but with a dominant super-ego, his inhibitions so extreme that it came out mainly as exaggerated dignity and precision in his movements. He almost never permitted himself any kind of open or prominent facial expression. But he was not a calm person. He did not speak or act in a nervous way, but there was a vibe of intense tension about him—I can remember him seeming to give off a slight hum when at rest. In hindsight, I suspect he was probably only a year or two from needing blood pressure medication when the accident occurred.

I remember being aware that my father's overall posture or bearing seemed unusual for a shorter man—many short men tend to stand ramrod straight, for understandable reasons—in terms of his seeming not slumped but more like slightly bent forward at the waist, at a slight angle, which added to the sense of tension or always walking into some kind of wind. I know that I wouldn't understand this prior to entering the Service and seeing the bearing of some of the older examiners who spend all day for years at a desk or Tingle table, leaning forward to examine tax returns, primarily to identify those that should be audited. In other words, it's the posture of someone whose daily work means sitting very still at a desk and working on something in a concentrated way for years on end.

I really know very little about the reality of my father's job and what-all it entailed, though I certainly now know what cost systems are.

On the face of it, my entering a career in the IRS might appear connected to my father's accident—in more humanistic terms, connected to my 'loss' of a father who was himself an accountant. My father's technical area was accounting systems and processes, which is actually closer to data processing than real accountancy, as I would later understand. For myself, however, I am convinced that I would now be in the Service regardless, given the dramatic event that I remember totally changing my focus and attitude which occurred the following fall, during the third semester of my returning to DePaul and when I was retaking Intro Accounting, along with American Political Theory, which was another class I'd gotten an incomplete in at Lindenhurst through basically not knuckling down and putting in the work. It's true, though, that I may have done this—retaking Intro Accounting—at least partly to please or try to pay back my father, or to at least lessen the self-disgust I had felt after his walking into the nihilistic scene in the living room which I just mentioned. It was probably only a couple days after that scene and my father's reaction that I took the CTA commuter line down to Lincoln Park and started trying to reenroll for my last two years—in terms of credits, four terms—at DePaul, although due to certain technicalities I couldn't officially reenter until the fall of '77—another long story—and, thanks to knuckling down and also swallowing my pride and getting some extra help to deal with depreciation and amortization schedules, finally did pass, along with DePaul's version of American Political Theory—which they called American Political Thought, although it and the Lindenhurst version of the course were nearly identical—in the Fall 1978 semester, though not exactly with final grades to write home about, because I largely neglected serious studying for these two classes' final exams due to (somewhat ironically) the dramatic event, which occurred accidentally during an entirely different DePaul class, one I was not even really taking but sort of bumbled into through an inattentive screw-up during the final review period just before Christmas break, and was so dramatically moved and affected by that I barely even studied for my regular courses' final exams, though this time not out of carelessness or sloth but because I decided I had some very important, sustained, concentrated thinking to do after the dramatic encounter with the substitute Jesuit in Advanced Tax, which was the class I've mentioned sitting in on by mistake.

The fact is that there are probably just certain kinds of people who are drawn to a career in the IRS. People who are, as the substitute father said that final day in Advanced Tax, 'called to account.' Meaning we are talking about almost a special kind of psychological type, probably. It's not a very common type—perhaps one in 10,000—but the thing is that the sort of person of this type who decides that he wants to enter the Service really, really wants to, and becomes very determined, and will be hard to put off course once he's focused in on his real vocation and begun to be actively drawn to it. And even one in 10,000, in a country as large as America, will add up to a fair number of people—roughly 20,000—for whom the IRS fulfills all the professional and psychological criteria for a real vocation. These twenty or so thousand comprise the Service's core, or heart, and not all of them are high-ranked in the IRS administration, although some of them are. These are 20,000 out of the Service's total of over 105,000 employees. And there are no doubt core characteristics that these people have in common, predictive factors which at some point or other kick in and cause a genuine calling to pursue tax accounting and systems administration and organizational behavior and to devote themselves to helping administer and enforce the tax laws of this country as spelled out in Title 26 of the Code of Federal Regulations and the Revised Internal Revenue Code of 1954, plus all the statutes and regulations entailed by the Tax Reform Act of 1969, the Tax Reform Act of 1976, the Revenue Act of 1978, and so on and so forth. What these reasons and factors are, and to what extent they coexist with the particular talents and dispositions the Service is in need of—these are interesting questions, which today's IRS takes an active interest in understanding and quantifying. In terms of myself and how I got here, the important thing is that I discovered I had them—the factors and characteristics—and discovered this suddenly, by what seemed at the time like nothing more than a feckless mistake.

I've left out the matter of recreational drug abuse during this period, and the relation of certain drugs to how I got here, which in no way represents an endorsement of drug abuse but is just part of the story of the factors that eventually drew me to the Service. But it's complicated, and somewhat indirect. It's obvious that drugs were a big part of the whole scene in this era—this is well-known. I remember in the later seventies, the supposedly coolest recreational drug around Chicagoland college campuses was cocaine, and given how anxious I was at that time to conform, I'm sure I would have used more cocaine, or 'coke,' if I'd liked the effects. But I didn't—like it, I mean. It didn't cause euphoric excitement for me, it more just made me feel as though I'd had a dozen cups of coffee on an empty stomach. It was a terrible feeling, even though people around me like Steve Edwards talked about cocaine as if it was the greatest feeling of all time. I didn't get it. I also didn't like the way it made the people who had just done cocaine's eyes bulge out and their lips move around on their face in strange, uncontrollable ways, and the way even shallow or obvious ideas suddenly seemed incredibly profound to them. My overall memory of this cocaine period was of being at some kind of party with someone on cocaine who kept talking to me in this very rapid, intense way, and of me trying to subtly back away, and of every time I take a step backwards they take a step forwards, and so on and so forth, until they've backed me against a wall of the party and my back is literally up against the wall and they're talking very fast only inches from my face, which was something I didn't like at all. This actually happened at parties during this period. I think I have some of my father's inhibition. Close bodily proximity to someone who's very excited or upset is something I've always had a difficult time with, which is one reason why the Audits Division was out of the question for me during the selection and posting phase at the TAC—which I should explain stands for 'Training and Assessment Center,' which roughly one quarter of today's Service's contract personnel above the grade of GS-9 have started out by attending, especially those who—like me—entered through a recruitment program. As of now, there are two such centers, one in Indianapolis and a slightly larger one in Columbus, OH. Both TACs are divisions of what is commonly known as Treasury School, as the Service is technically a branch of the US Treasury Department. But Treasury also includes everything from the Bureau of Alcohol, Tobacco, and

Firearms to the US Secret Service, so 'Treasury School'
now stands for over a dozen different training programs
and facilities, including the Federal Law Enforcement
Academy in Athens, GA, to which those posted to Criminal Investigations from the TAC are sent for specialized
training which they share with ATF agents, the DEA, federal marshals, and so on and so forth.

Anyhow, downers like Seconal and Valium simply
made me go to sleep and sleep through whatever noise,
including alarm clocks, happened to occur for the next
fourteen hours, so these were not high on my list of favorites, either. You have to understand that most of these
drugs were both plentiful and easy to get during this
period. This was especially true at UIC, where the roommate I watched the foot and hung out so frequently at the
Hat with was something of a human vending machine of
recreational drugs, having established connections with
mid-level dealers in the western suburbs, whom he always
got extremely paranoid and suspicious if you asked him
anything about, as if these were mafiosi instead of usually
just young couples in apartment complexes. I know one
thing he liked about me, though, as a roommate, was that
there were so many different types of drugs that I didn't
like or that didn't agree with me that he didn't have to be
constantly worried about my discovering his stash—which
he usually kept in two guitar cases in the back of his half
of the closet, which any idiot could have figured out from
his behavior with the closet or the number of cases he had
back there versus the one guitar he actually brought out
and played his two songs over and over with—or ripping
him off. Like most student dealers, he did not deal cocaine,

as there was too much money involved, not to mention coked-out people pounding on your door at 3:00 in the morning, so that cocaine was handled more by slightly older guys in leather hats and tiny little rat-like mustaches who operated out of bars like the Hat and King Philip's, which was another fashionable pub of the period, near the Mercantile Exchange on Monroe, where they also serviced younger commodity traders.

The UIC roommate was usually generously stocked in psychedelics, which by that time had definitely passed into the mainstream, but personally psychedelics frightened me, mostly because of what I remembered happening to Art Linkletter's daughter—my parents had been very into watching Art Linkletter in my childhood.

Like any normal college student, I liked alcohol, especially beer in bars, though I didn't like drinking so much that I got sick—being nauseated is something I essentially can't stand. I'd much rather be in pain than sick to my stomach. But I also, like almost everyone else who wasn't an evangelical Christian or part of Campus Crusade, liked marijuana, which in the Chicagoland area during that period was called pot or 'blow.' (Cocaine was not called blow by anyone I ever knew, and only hippie posers ever called pot 'grass,' which had been the hip sixties term but was now out of fashion.) This pot usage had peaked during high school, but I still sometimes smoked pot in college, although I suspect this was largely a matter of just doing what everyone else did—at Lindenhurst, for instance, almost everyone smoked marijuana constantly, including openly on the south quad on Wednesdays, which everyone called 'hash Wednesday.' I should add that now that

I am with the IRS, of course, my pot-smoking days are long behind me. For one thing, the Service is technically a law enforcement agency, and it would be hypocritical and wrong. Relatedly, the whole culture of the Examinations Division is inimical to smoking pot, as even rote exams requires a very sharp, organized, and methodical type of mental state, with the ability to concentrate for long periods of time, and, even more important, the ability to choose what one concentrates on versus ignoring, an ability which smoking marijuana would all but destroy.

There was, however, sporadically throughout this whole period, the matter of Obetrol, which is chemically related to Dexedrine but did not have the horrible breath and taste-in-the-mouth thing of Dexedrine. It was also related to Ritalin, but much easier to get, as Obetrol was the prescription appetite suppressant of choice for overweight women for several years in the mid-seventies, and which I liked very much, somewhat for the same reasons I'd liked Ritalin so much that one time, though also partly—in this later period, with me five years older than high school—for other reasons which are harder to explain. My affinity for Obetrol had to do with self-awareness, which I used to privately call 'doubling.' It's hard to explain. Take pot, for instance—some people report that smoking it makes them paranoid. For me, though, although I liked pot in some situations, the problem was more specific—smoking pot made me self-conscious, sometimes so much so that it made it difficult to be around people. This was another reason why smoking pot with my mother and Joyce was so awkward and tense—the truth is that I actually preferred to smoke pot by myself, and was much more comfortable with pot if I could be high by myself and just sort of space out. I'm mentioning this as a contrast with Obetrol, which you could either take as a regular capsule or untwist the halves of and crush the tiny little beads into powder and snort it up with a straw or rolled bill, rather like cocaine. Snorting Obetrols burns the inside of the nose something terrible, though, so I tended to prefer the old-fashioned way, when I took them, which I used to privately refer to as Obetrolling. It's not like I went around constantly Obetrolling, by the way—they were more recreational, and not always easy to get, depending on whether the overweight girls you knew at a given college or dorm were serious about dieting or not, which some were and some weren't, as with anything. One coed that I got them from for almost a whole year at DePaul wasn't even very overweight—her mother sent them to her, along with cookies she'd baked, weirdly—evidently the mother had some serious psychological conflicts about food and weight that she tried to project onto the daughter, who was not exactly a fox but was definitely cool and blasé about her mother's neurosis about her weight, and more or less said, 'Whatever,' and was content to offload the Obetrols for two dollars apiece and to share the cookies with her roommate. There was also one guy in the high-rise dorm on Roosevelt who took them by prescription, for narcolepsy—sometimes he would just fall asleep in the middle of whatever he was doing, and he took Obetrol out of medical necessity, since they were evidently very good for narcolepsy—and he would every once in a while give a couple away if he was in an expansive mood, but he never actually sold or dealt them—he believed it was bad karma. But for the most part, they were not hard to get, although the roommate from UIC never carried Obetrols for sale and squeezed my shoes about liking them, referring to the stimulants as 'Mother's little helper' and saying that anyone who wanted them could just ring the doorbell of any overweight housewife in the Chicagoland area, which was obviously an exaggeration. But they were not all that popular. There weren't even any street names or euphemisms for them—if you were looking for them, you had to just say the brand name, which for some reason seemed terribly uncool, and not enough people I knew were into them to make *Obetrolling* any kind of candidate for a hip term.

The reason I bring up pot is for contrast. Obetrolling didn't make me self-conscious. But it did make me much more self-aware. If I was in a room, and had taken an Obetrol or two with a glass of water and they'd taken effect, I was now not only in the room, but I was aware that I was in the room. In fact, I remember I would often think, or say to myself, quietly but very clearly, *'I am in this room.'* It's difficult to explain this. At the time, I called it 'doubling,' but I'm still not entirely sure what I meant by this, nor why it seemed so profound and cool to not only be in a room but be totally aware that I was in the room, seated in a certain easy chair in a certain position listening to a certain specific track of an album whose cover was a certain specific combination of colors and designs—being in a state of heightened enough awareness to be able to consciously say to myself, *'I am in this room right now. The shadow of the foot is rotating on the east wall. The shadow is not recognizable as a foot because of the deformation of the angle of the light of the sun's position behind the sign. I am seated upright in a dark-green easy chair with a cigarette burn on the right armrest. The cigarette burn is black and imperfectly round. The track I am listening to is "The Big Ship" off of Brian Eno's* Another Green World, *whose cover has colorful cutout figures inside a white frame.'* Stated so openly, this amount of detail might seem tedious, but it wasn't. What it felt like was a sort of emergence, however briefly, from the fuzziness and drift of my life in that period. As though I was a machine that suddenly realized it was a human being and didn't have to just go through the motions it was programmed to perform over and over. It also had to do with paying attention. It wasn't like the normal thing with recreational drugs which made colors brighter or music more intense. What became more intense was my awareness of my own part in it, that I could pay real attention to it. It was that I could look at, for instance, a dorm room's walls of institutional tan or beige and not only see them but be aware that I was seeing them—this was the dorm at UIC—and that I normally lived within these walls and was probably affected in all kinds of subtle ways by their institutional color but was usually unaware of how they made me feel, unaware of what it felt like to look at them, unaware usually of even their color and texture, because I never really looked at anything in a precise, attentive way. It was kind of striking. Their texture was mostly smooth, but if you really focused your attention there were also a lot of the little embedded strings and clots which painters tend to leave when they're paid by the job and not the hour and thus have motivation to hurry. If you really look at something, you can almost always tell what type of wage structure the person who made it was on. Or of the shadow of the sign and the way that the placement and height of the sun at the time affected the shape of the shadow, which mainly appeared to contract and expand as the real sign rotated across the street, or of the way that turning the little desk lamp next to the chair on and off changed the room's interplay of light and the different objects in the room's shadows and even the specific shade of the walls and ceiling and affected everything, and—through the 'doubling'—also being aware that I was turning the lamp off and on and noticing the changes and being affected by them, and by the fact that I knew I was noticing them. That I was aware of the awareness. It maybe sounds abstract or stoned, but it isn't. To me, it felt alive. There was something about it I preferred. I could listen to Floyd, say, or even one of the roommate's constant records from his bedroom like *Sgt. Pepper,* and not only hear the music and each note and bar and key change and resolution of each track, but know, with the same kind of awareness and discrimination, that I was doing this, meaning really listening—*'Right now I am listening to the second chorus of the Beatles' "Fixing a Hole"'*—but also being aware of the exact feelings and sensations the music produced in me. That may sound all drippy-hippie, getting in touch with inner feelings and all that business. But based on my experience during that time, most people are always feeling something or adopting some attitude or choosing to pay attention to one thing or one part of something without even knowing we're doing it. We do it automatically, like a heartbeat. Sometimes I'd be sitting there in a room and become aware of how much effort it was to pay attention to just your own heartbeat for more than a minute or so—it's almost as though your heartbeat wants to stay out of awareness, like a rock star avoiding the limelight. But it's there if you can double up and make yourself pay attention. Same with music, too, the doubling was being able to both listen very closely and also to feel whatever emotions the music evoked—because obviously that's why we're into music, that it makes us feel certain things, otherwise it would just be noise—and not only have them, listening, but be aware of them, to be able to say to yourself, *'This song is making me feel both warm and safe, as though cocooned like a little boy that's just been taken out of the bath and wrapped in towels that have been washed so many times they're incredibly soft, and also at the same time feeling sad; there's an emptiness at the center of the warmth like the way an empty church or classroom with a lot of windows through which you can only see rain on the street is sad, as though right at the center of this safe, enclosed feeling is the seed of emptiness.'* Not that you'd necessarily say it that way, just that it was distinct and palpable enough to be said that specifically, if you wanted to. And being aware of that distinctness, as well. Anyhow, this was why I was into Obetrol. The point wasn't just to zone out on pretty music or back somebody up against a party wall.

And nor was it just good or pleasurable things you were aware of, on Obetrol or Cylert. Some of the stuff it brought into awareness wasn't pleasant, it was just reality. Like sitting in the UIC dorm room's little living room and listening to the roommate-slash-social-rebel from Naperville in his bedroom talking on his phone—this so-called nonconformist had his own phone line, paid for by guess who—talking to some coed, which if there was no music or TV on, you couldn't help overhearing through the walls, which were notoriously easy to put your fist through if you were the type that punched walls, and listening to his rap of ingratiating patter to this coed, and not only sort of disliking him and feeling embarrassed for him at the affected way he talked to girls—as if anybody who was paying any attention could miss seeing how hard he was trying to project this idea of himself as hip and radical without being the slightest bit aware of how it really looked, which was spoiled, insecure, and vain—and listening and feeling all this, but also being uncomfortably aware that I was, meaning having to consciously feel and be aware of these inner reactions instead of just having them operate in me without quite admitting them to myself. I don't think I'm explaining it very well. Like having to be able to say to yourself, '*I am pretending to sit here reading Albert Camus's* The Fall *for the Literature of Alienation midterm, but actually I'm really concentrating on listening to Steve try to impress this girl over the phone, and I am feeling embarrassment and contempt for him, and am thinking he's a poser, and at the same time I am also uncomfortably aware of times that I've also tried to project the idea of myself as hip and cynical so as to impress someone, meaning that not only do I sort of dislike Steve, which in all honesty I do, but part of the reason I dislike him is that when I listen to him on the phone it makes me see similarities and realize things about myself that embarrass me, but I don't know how to quit doing them—like, if I quit trying to seem nihilistic, even just to myself, then what would happen, what would I be like? And will I even remember this when I'm not Obetrolling, or will I just go back to being irritated by Steve Edwards without quite letting myself be aware of it, or why?*' Does this make sense? It could be frightening, because I would see all this with uncomfortable clarity, although I would not have used a word like *nihilism* during that period without trying to make it sound cool or like an allusion, which to myself, in the clarity of doubling, I wouldn't have been tempted to do, as I did things like this only when I wasn't really aware of what I was doing or what my real agenda was, but rather on some kind of strange, robotic autopilot. Which, when I did Obetrol—or once, at DePaul, a variant called Cylert, which only came in 10 mg. tablets, and was only available one time in a very special situation that never repeated—I tended to realize again that I wasn't even really aware of what was going on, most of the time. Like taking the train instead of actually driving yourself somewhere and having to know where you were and make decisions about where to turn. On the train, one can simply space out and ride along, which is what it felt as though I was doing most of the time. And I'd be aware of this too, on these stimulants, and aware of the fact that I was aware. The awarenesses were fleeting, though, and after I came off of the Obetrol—which usually involved a bad headache—afterward, it felt as though I barely remembered any of the things I'd become aware of. The memory of the feeling of suddenly coming awake and being aware felt vague and diffuse, like something you think you see at the outer periphery of your vision but then can't see when you try to look directly at it. Or like a fragment of memory which you're not sure whether it was real or part of a dream. Just as I'd predicted and been afraid of when I'd been doubled, of course. So it wasn't all fun and games, which was one reason why Obetrolling felt true and important instead of just goofy and pleasurable like pot. Some of it was uncomfortably vivid. As in not merely waking up to an awareness of my dislike of the roommate and his denim workshirts and guitar and all of the so-called friends who came around and had to pretend to like him and find him cool in order to get their gram of hash from him or whatever, and not just disliking the whole rooming situation and even the nihilistic ritual of the foot and the Hat, which we pretended was a lot cooler and funnier than it was—as it wasn't as though we did it just once or twice but basically all the time, it was really just an excuse not to study or do our work and instead be wastoids while our parents paid our tuition, room, and board—but also being aware, when I really looked at it, that part of me had chosen to room with Steve Edwards because part of me actually sort of enjoyed disliking him and cataloguing things about him that were hypocritical and made me feel a sort of embarrassed distaste, and that there must be certain psychological reasons why I lived, ate, partied, and hung around with a person I didn't even really like or respect very much . . . which probably meant that I didn't respect myself very much, either, and that was why I was such a conformist. And the point is that, sitting there overhearing Steve tell the girl on the phone that he'd always felt today's women had to be seen as more than just sex objects if there was going to be any hope for the human race, I would be articulating all this to myself, very clearly and consciously, instead of just drifting around having all these sensations and reactions about him without ever being quite aware of them. So it basically meant waking up to how unaware I normally was, and knowing that I'd be going back to sleep like that when the artificial effect of the speed wore off. Meaning it wasn't all fun and games. But it did feel *alive,* and that's probably why I liked it. It felt like I actually *owned* myself. Instead of renting or whatever—I don't know. But that analogy sounds too cheap, like a cheap witticism. It's hard to explain, and this is probably more time than I should take to explain it. Nor am I obviously trying to give any pro-drug-abuse message here. But it was important. I like now to think of the Obetrol and other subtypes of speed as more of a kind of signpost or directional sign, pointing to what might be possible if I could become more aware and alive in daily life. In this sense, I think that abusing these drugs was a valuable experience for me, as I was basically so feckless and unfocused during this period that I needed a very clear, blunt type of hint that there was much more to being an alive, responsible, autonomous adult than I had any idea of at the time.

On the other hand, it goes without saying the key is moderation. You couldn't spend all your time taking Obetrols and sitting there doubled and aware and still expect to take care of business effectively. I remember not getting Camus's *The Fall* read in time, for instance, and having to totally bullshit my way through the Literature of Alienation midterm—in other words, I was cheating, at least by implication—but not feeling much about it one way or the other, that I can recall, except a sort of cynical, disgusted relief when the prof's grader wrote something like 'Interesting in places!' under the B. Meaning a meaningless bullshit response to meaningless bullshit. But there was no denying it was powerful—the feeling that everything important was right there and I could sometimes wake up almost in mid-stride, in the middle of all the meaningless bullshit, and suddenly be aware of it. It's hard to explain. The truth is that I think the Obetrol and doubling was my first glimmer of the sort of impetus that I believe helped lead me into the Service and the special problems and priorities here at the Regional Examination Center. It had something to do with paying attention and the ability to choose what I paid attention to, and to be aware of that choice, the fact that it's a choice. I'm not the smartest person, but even during that whole pathetic, directionless period, I think that deep down I knew that there was more to my life and to myself than just the ordinary psychological impulses for pleasure and vanity that I let drive me. That there were depths to me that were not bullshit or childish but profound, and were not abstract but actually much realer than my clothes or self-image, and that blazed in an almost sacred way—I'm being serious; I'm not just trying to make it sound more dramatic than it was—and that these realest, most profound parts of me involved not drives or appetites but simple attention, awareness, if only I could stay awake off speed.

But I couldn't. As mentioned, usually afterwards I couldn't even recall what had seemed so clear and profound about what I'd come to be aware of in that cheap green previous tenant's easy chair, which somebody had just left there in the room when he'd moved out of the dorm, and which had something broken or bent in its frame under the cushions and kind of tilted to one side when you tried to lean back, so you had to sit up very straight and erect in it, which was an odd feeling. The whole doubling incident would be covered with a sort of mental fuzz the next morning, especially if I woke up late—which I usually did, given what was essentially a kind of amphetamine's effects on getting to sleep—and had to more or less hit the floor running and hurry to class without even noticing anyone or anything I was running past. In essence, I was one of those types that have a terror of being late but still always seem to be running late. If I came into something late I'd often be too tense and wound up at first even to be able to follow what was going on. I know I inherited the fear of lateness from my father. Plus, it's true that sometimes the heightened awareness and self-articulation of doubling on Obetrols could go too far—'*Now I am aware that I am aware that I'm sitting up oddly straight, now I'm aware that I feel an itch on the left side of my neck, now I'm aware that I'm deliberating whether to scratch or not, now I'm aware of paying attention to that deliberation and what the ambivalence about scratching feels like and what those feelings and my awareness of them do to my awareness of the intensity of the itch.*' Meaning that past a certain point, the element of choice of attention in doubling could get lost, and the awareness could sort of explode into a hall of mirrors of consciously felt sensations and thoughts and awareness of awareness of awareness of these. This was attention without choice, meaning the loss of the ability to focus in and concentrate on just one thing, and was another big incentive for moderation in the use of Obetrols, especially late at night—I have to admit that I know that once or twice I got so lost in the halls or stacked layers of awareness of awareness that I went to the bathroom right there on the sofa—this was up at Lindenhurst College, where there were three roommates per suite and a semi-furnished 'social room' in the suite's center, where the sofa was—which, even at the time, seemed like a clear sign of loss of basic priorities and failure to take care of business. For some reason now, I sometimes have a mental picture of me trying to explain to my father how I somehow became so totally focused and aware that I sat there and wet my pants, but the picture cuts off just as his mouth opens for a response, and I'm 99 percent sure this is not a real memory—how could he know anything about a davenport all the way up in Lindenhurst?

For the record, it is true that I miss my father and was very upset about what happened, and sometimes I feel quite sad at the thought that he is not here to see the career path I've chosen, and the changes in me as a person as a result, and some of my PP-47 performance evaluations, and to talk about cost systems and forensic accounting with from a vastly more adult perspective.

And yet these flickers of deeper awareness, whether drug-induced or not—for it is arguable how much that ultimately matters—probably had more of a direct effect on my life and direction's change and my entering the Service in 1979 than did my father's accident, or possibly even more than the dramatic experience I underwent in the Advanced Tax review class that I had sat in on by mistake during my second, ultimately much more focused and successful enrollment at DePaul. I've mentioned this mistaken final review already. In a nutshell, the story of this experience is that DePaul's Lincoln Park campus had two newer buildings that looked very alike, were literally almost mirror images of one another, by architectural design, and were connected at both the first floor and—by an overhead transom not unlike our own at the Midwest REC—at the third floor, and DePaul's accounting and political science departments were in the two different buildings of this identical set, whose names I don't recall at this moment. Meaning the buildings' names. It was the last regular class day for Tuesday–Thursday classes of the Fall '78 term, and we were to be reviewing for the final exam in American Political Thought, which was to be all essay questions, and on my way to the final review I know I was trying to mentally review the areas that I wanted to make sure at least someone in the class asked about—it didn't have to be me—in terms of how extensively they would be covered on the final. Except for Intro Accounting, I was still taking mostly psychology and political science classes—the latter ones mostly due to the requirements for declaring a major, which you had to satisfy in order to graduate—but now that I wasn't merely trying to squeak by on last-minute bullshit, these classes were obviously much harder and more time-consuming. I remember that most of DePaul's version of American Political Thought was on *The Federalist Papers,* by Madison et al., which I had had before at Lindenhurst but remembered almost none of. In essence, I was so intent on thinking about the review and the final exam that what happened is that I took the wrong building entrance without noticing it, and ended up in the correct third-floor room but the wrong building, with this room being such an identical mirror image of the adjoining building's correct room, directly across the transom, that I didn't immediately notice the error. And this classroom turned out to contain the final review day of Advanced Tax, a famously difficult course at DePaul that was known as the accounting department's equivalent of what organic chemistry was for science majors—the final hurdle, the weed-out class, requiring several prerequisites and open to senior accounting majors and postgrads only, and said to be taught by one of DePaul's few remaining Jesuit professors, meaning with the official black-and-white clothing ensemble and absolutely zero sense of humor or desire to be liked or 'connecting' with the students. At DePaul, the Jesuits were notoriously unmellow. My father, by the way, was raised as a Roman Catholic but had little or nothing to do with the church as an adult. My mom's family was originally Lutheran. Like many of my generation, I wasn't raised as anything. But this day in the identical classroom also turned out to be one of the most unexpectedly powerful, galvanizing events of my life at that time, and made such an impression that I even remember what I was wearing as I sat there—a red-and-brown-striped acrylic sweater, white painter's pants, and Timberland boots whose color my roommate—who was a serious chemistry major, no more Steve Edwardses and rotating feet—called 'dogshit yellow,' with the laces untied and dragging, which was the way everyone I knew or hung out with wore their Timberlands that year.

By the way, I do think that awareness is different from thinking. I am similar to most other people, I believe, in that I do not really do my most important thinking in large, intentional blocks where I sit down uninterrupted in a chair and know in advance what it is I'm going to think about—as in, for instance, *'I am going to think about life and my place in it and what's truly important to me, so that I can start forming concrete, focused goals and plans for my adult career'*—and then sit there and think about it until I reach a conclusion. It doesn't work like that. For myself, I tend to do my most important thinking in incidental, accidental, almost daydreamy ways. Making a sandwich, taking a shower, sitting in a wrought-iron chair in the Lakehurst mall food court waiting for someone who's late, riding the CTA train and staring at both the passing scene and my own faint reflection superimposed on it in the window—and suddenly you find you're thinking about things that end up being important. It's almost the opposite of awareness, if you think about it. I think this experience of accidental thinking is common, if perhaps not universal, although it's not something that you can ever really talk to anyone else about because it ends up being so abstract and hard to explain. Whereas in an intentional bout of concentrated major thinking, where you sit down with the conscious intention of confronting major questions like *'Am I currently happy?'* or *'What, ultimately, do I really care about and believe in?'* or—particularly if some kind of authority figure has just squeezed your shoes—*'Am I essentially a worthwhile, contributing type of person or a drifting, indifferent, nihilistic person?,'* then the questions often end up not answered but more like beaten to death, so attacked from every angle and each angle's different objections and complications that they end up even more abstract and ultimately meaningless than when you started. Nothing is achieved this way, at least that I've ever heard of. Certainly, from all evidence, St. Paul, or Martin Luther, or the authors of *The Federalist Papers,* or even President Reagan never changed the direction of their lives this way—it happened more by accident.

53

As for my father, I have to admit that I don't know how he did any of the major thinking that led him in the directions he followed all his life. I don't even know whether there *was* any major, conscious thinking in his case. Like many men of his generation, he may well have been one of those people who can just proceed on autopilot. His attitude towards life was that there are certain things that have to be done and you simply have to do them—such as, for instance, going to work every day. Again, it may be that this is another element of the generation gap. I don't think my father loved his job with the city, but on the other hand, I'm not sure he ever asked himself major questions like '*Do I like my job? Is this really what I want to spend my life doing? Is it as fulfilling as some of the dreams I had for myself when I was a young man serving in Korea and reading British poetry in my bunk in the barracks at night?*' He had a family to support, this was his job, he got up every day and did it, end of story, everything else is just self-indulgent nonsense. That may actually have been the lifetime sum-total of his thinking on the matter. He essentially said 'Whatever' to his lot in life, but obviously in a very different way from the way in which the directionless wastoids of my generation said 'Whatever.'

My mother, on the other hand, changed her life's direction very dramatically—but again, I don't know whether this was as a result of concentrated thinking. In fact, I doubt it. That is just not how things like this work. The truth is that most of my mother's choices were emotionally driven. This was another common dynamic for her generation. I think that she liked to believe that the feminist consciousness-raising and Joyce and the whole thing of her and Joyce and the divorce were the result of thinking, like a conscious change of life-philosophy. But it was really emotional. She had a sort of nervous breakdown in 1971, even though nobody ever used that term. And maybe she would eschew 'nervous breakdown' and say instead that it was a sudden, conscious change in beliefs and direction. And who can really argue with something like that? I wish I had understood this at the time, because there were ways in which I know I was kind of nasty and condescending to my mother about the whole Joyce and divorce thing. Almost as though I unconsciously sided with my father, and took it upon myself to say all the nasty, condescending things that he was too self-disciplined and dignified to allow himself to say. Even speculating about it is probably pointless—as my father said, people are going to do what they're going to do, and all you can really do is play the hand that life deals you to the best of your ability. I never knew with any certainty whether he even really missed her, or was sad. When I think of him now, I realize he was lonely, that it was very hard for him divorced and alone in that house in Libertyville. After the divorce, in some ways he probably felt free, which of course has its good sides—he could come and go as he pleased, and when he squeezed my shoes about something he didn't have to worry about choosing his words carefully or arguing with someone who was going to stick up for me no matter what. But freedom of this kind is also very close, on the psychological continuum, to loneliness. The only people you're really ultimately 'free' with in this way are strangers, and in this sense my father was right about money and capitalism being equal to freedom, as buying or selling something doesn't obligate you to anything except what's written in the contract—although there's also the social contract, which is where the obligation to pay one's fair share of taxes comes in, and I think my father would have agreed with Mr. Glendenning's statement that 'Real freedom is freedom to obey the law.' That all probably doesn't make much sense. Anyhow, it's all just abstract speculation at this point, because I never really talked to either of my parents about how they felt about their adult lives. It's just not the sort of thing that parents sit down and openly discuss with their children, at least not in that era.

Anyhow, it would probably help to provide some background info. The easiest way to define a tax is to say that the amount of the tax, symbolized as T, is equal to the product of the tax base and tax rate. This is usually symbolized as $T = B \times R$, so you can then get $R = T/B$, which is the formula for determining whether a tax rate is progressive, regressive, or proportional. This is very basic tax accounting. It is so familiar to most IRS personnel that we don't even have to think about it. But anyhow, the critical variable is T's relationship to B. If the ratio of T to B stays the same regardless of whether B, the tax base, goes up or down, then the tax is proportional. This is also known as a flat-rate tax. A progressive tax is where the ratio T/B increases as B increases and decreases as B decreases—which is essentially the way today's marginal income tax works, in which you pay 0 percent on your first 2,300 dollars, 14 percent on your next 1,100 dollars, 16 percent on your next 1,000, and so on and so forth, up to 70 percent of everything over $108,300, which is all part of the US Treasury's current policy that, in theory, the more annual income you have, the greater the proportion of your income your income tax obligation should represent—although obviously it does not always work this way in practice, given all of the various legal deductions and credits which are part of the modern tax code. Anyhow, progressive tax schedules can be symbolized by a simple ascending bar graph, each bar of which represents a given tax bracket. Sometimes a progressive tax is also called a graduated tax, but this is not the Service's term for it. A regressive tax, on the other hand, is where the ratio T/B increases as B decreases, meaning you pay the highest tax rates on the smallest amounts, which arguably doesn't make much sense in terms of fairness and the social contract. However, regressive taxes can often appear in disguise—for instance, opponents of state lotteries and cigarette taxes often claim that what these things amount to is a disguised regressive tax. The Service has no opinion on this issue either way. Anyhow, income taxes are almost always progressive, given our country's democratic ideals. Here, on the other hand, are some of the types of taxes which are usually proportional or flat: real property, personal property, customs, excise, and especially sales tax.

As many people here remember, in 1977, during high inflation, high deficits, and my second enrollment at DePaul, there was a state fiscal experiment in Illinois in which the state sales tax was to be made progressive instead of proportional. This was probably my first experience of seeing how the implementation of tax policy can actually affect people's lives. As mentioned, sales taxes are normally almost universally proportional. As I now understand it, the idea behind trying a progressive sales tax was to raise state tax revenues while not inflicting hardship on the state's poor or discouraging investors, plus also to help combat inflation by taxing consumption. The idea was that the more you bought, the more tax you paid, which would help discourage demand and ease inflation. The progressive sales tax was the brainchild of someone high up in the State Treasurer's Office in 1977. Just who this person was, or whether he wore the brown helmet in some way after the resulting disaster, I do not know, but both the state treasurer and the governor of Illinois definitely lost their jobs over the fiasco. Whoever's fault it ultimately was, though, it was a major tax-policy boner, which actually could have been easily prevented if anyone in the State Treasurer's Office had bothered to consult with the Service about the advisability of the scheme. Despite the existence of both the Midwest Regional Commissioner's Office and a Regional Examination Center within Illinois's borders, however, it's an established fact that this never occurred. Despite state revenue agencies' reliance on federal tax returns and the Service's computer system's master files in the enforcement of state tax law, there is a tradition of autonomy and distrust among state revenue offices for federal agencies like the IRS, which sometimes results in key communication lapses, of which the 1977 Illinois sales tax disaster is, within the Service, a classic case, and the subject of numerous professional jokes and stories. As almost anyone here at Post 047 could have told them, a fundamental rule of effective tax enforcement is remembering that the average taxpayer is always going to act out of his own monetary self-interest. This is basic economic law. In taxation, the result is that the taxpayer will always do whatever the law allows him to do in order to minimize his taxes. This is simple human nature, which the Illinois officials either failed to understand or neglected to see the implications of for sales tax transactions. It may be a case of the State Treasurer's Office allowing the whole matter to get so complex and theoretical that they failed to see what was right in front of their nose—the base, B, of a progressive tax cannot be something which can be easily subdivided. If it can be easily subdivided, then the average taxpayer, acting out of his own economic interest, will do whatever he can legally do to subdivide the B into two or more smaller Bs in order to avoid the effective progression. And this, in late 1977, was precisely what happened. The result was retail chaos. At, for instance, the supermarket, shoppers would no longer purchase three large bags of groceries for $78 total and submit to paying 6, 6.8, and 8.5 percent on those parts of their purchases over $5.00, $20.00, and $42.01, respectively—they were now motivated to structure their grocery purchase as numerous separate small purchases of $4.99 or less in order to take advantage of the much more attractive 3.75 percent sales tax on purchases under $5.00. The difference between 8 percent and 3.75 percent is more than enough to establish incentive and make citizens' economic self-interest kick in. So, at the store, you suddenly had everyone buying under $5.00 worth of groceries and running out to their car and putting the little bag in the car and running back in and buying another amount under $5.00 and running out to their car, and so on and so forth. Supermarkets' checkout lines started going all the way to the back of the store. Department stores were just as bad, and I know gas stations were even worse—only a few months after the supply shock of OPEC and fights in gas lines over rationing, now, in Illinois that autumn, fights also broke out at gas stations from drivers being forced to wait as people ahead of them at the pump tried putting $4.99 worth in and running in and paying and running back out and resetting the pump and putting in another $4.99, and so on. It was the exact opposite of mellow, to say the least. And the administrative burden of calculating sales tax over four separate margins of purchases just about broke retail stores. Those with automated registers and bookkeeping systems saw the systems crash under the new load. From what I understand, the high administrative costs of the new bookkeeping burden got passed along and caused an inflationary spike in Illinois, which then further aggrieved consumers who were already peeved because the progressive sales tax was economically forcing them to go through checkout lines half a dozen times or more, in many cases. There were some riots, especially in the southern part of the state, which abuts Kentucky and tends not to be what you'd call understanding or sympathetic about government's need to collect revenue in the first place. The truth is that northern, central, and southern Illinois are practically different countries, culturally speaking. But the chaos was statewide. The state treasurer was burnt in effigy. Banks saw a run on ones and change. From the perspective of administrative costs, the worst part came when enterprising businesses saw a new opportunity and started using 'Subdividable!' as a sales inducement. Including, for instance, used-car dealers that were willing to sell you a car as an agglomeration of separate little transactions for front bumper, right rear wheel well, alternator coil, spark plug, and so on, the purchase structured as thousands of different $4.99 transactions. It was technically legal, of course, and other big-ticket retailers soon followed—but I think it was when Realtors also got into the practice of subdividing that things really fell apart. Banks, mortgage brokers, dealers in commodities and bonds, and the Illinois Department of Revenue all saw their data processing systems buckle—the progressive sales tax produced a veritable tidal wave of subdivided-sales information that drowned the existing technology. The whole thing was repealed after less than four months. Actually, the state legislators came back to Springfield from their Christmas recess in order to convene and repeal it, as that period had been the most disastrous for retail commerce—holiday-season shopping in 1977 was a nightmare that people still sometimes chat ruefully about with strangers when they become stuck in checkout lines here in the state even now, years later. Rather the same way extreme heat or mugginess will make people reminisce together about other terrible summers they both remember. Springfield is the state capital, by the way, as well as the site of an incredible amount of Lincoln memorabilia.

Anyhow, it was also at this time that my father was killed unexpectedly in a CTA subway accident in Chicago, during the almost indescribably horrible and chaotic holiday shopping rush of December 1977, and the accident actually occurred while he was in the process of weekend Christmas shopping, which probably helped contribute to making the whole thing even more tragic. The accident was not on the famous 'El' part of the CTA—he and I were in the Washington Square station, to which we'd ridden in from Libertyville on the commuter line in order to transfer to a subway line going further downtown. I think we were ultimately headed to the Art Institute gift shop. I was back at my father's house for the weekend, I remember, at least partly because I had intensive studying to do for my first round of final exams since reenrolling at DePaul, where I was living in a dorm on the Loop campus. In retrospect, part of the reason for coming home to Libertyville to cram may also have been to give my father an opportunity to watch me apply myself to serious studying on a weekend, though I don't remember being aware of this motivation at the time. Also, for those who do not know, the Chicago Transit Authority's train system is a mishmash of elevated, conventional underground, and high-speed commuter rails. By prior agreement, I came into the city with him on Saturday in order to help him find some kind of Christmas gift for my mother and Joyce—a task I imagine he must have found difficult every year—and also, I think, for his sister, who lives with her husband and children in Fair Oaks, OK.

Essentially, what happened in the Washington Square station, where we were transferring downtown, is that we descended the cement steps of the subway level into the dense crowds and heat of the platform—even in December, Chicago's subway tunnels tend to be hot, although not nearly as unbearable as during the summer months, but, on the other hand, the platforms' winter heat is undergone while wearing a winter coat and scarf, and it was also extremely crowded, it being the holiday shopping rush, with the additional frenzy and chaos of the progressive sales tax being under way this year as well. Anyhow, I remember that we reached the bottom of the stairs and the platform's crowds just as the train slid in—it was stainless steel and tan plastic, with both full and partially pulled-off holly decals around some of the cars' windows—and the automatic doors opened with a pneumatic sound, and the train stood idling for the moment as large masses of impatient, numerous-small-purchase-laden holiday shoppers pushed on and off. In terms of crowdedness, it was also the peak shopping hours of Saturday afternoon. My father had wanted to do the shopping in the morning before the downtown crowds got completely out of control, but I had overslept, and he had waited for me, although he was not pleased about it and did not disguise this. We finally left after lunch—meaning, in my case, breakfast—and even on the commuter line into the city, the crowds had been intense. Now we arrived on the even more crowded platform at a moment that most subway riders will acknowledge as awkward and somewhat stressful, with the train idling and the doors open but one never knowing for sure how much longer they'll stay that way as you move through the platform's crowds, trying to get to the train before the doors close. You don't quite want to break into a run or start shoving people out of the way, as the more rational part of you knows it's hardly a matter of life and death, that another train will be along soon, and that the worst that can happen is that you'll barely miss it, that the doors will slide shut just as you get to the train, and you will have barely missed getting on and will have to wait on the hot, crowded platform for a few minutes. And yet there's always another part of you—or of me, anyhow, and I'm quite sure, in hindsight, of my father—which almost panics. The idea of the doors closing and the train with its crowds of people

who did make it inside pulling away just as you get up
to the doors provokes some kind of strange, involuntary
feeling of anxiety or urgency—I don't think there's even
a specific word for it, psychologically, though possibly it's
related to primal, prehistoric fears that you would somehow miss getting to eat your fair share of the tribe's kill or
would be caught out alone in the veldt's tall grass as night
falls—and, though he and I had certainly never talked
about it, I now suspect that this deep, involuntary sense
of anxiety about getting to idling trains just in time was
especially bad for my father, who was a man of extreme
organization and personal discipline and precise schedules
who was always precisely on time for everything, and for
whom the primal anxiety of just barely missing something
was especially intense—although on the other hand he was
also a man of enormous personal dignity and composure,
and would normally never allow himself to be seen shoul-
dering people aside or running on a public platform with
his topcoat billowing and one hand holding his dark-gray
hat down on his head and his keys and assorted pocket
change audibly jingling, not unless he felt some kind of
intense, irrational pressure to make the train, the way it
is often the most disciplined, organized, dignified people
who, it turns out, are under the most intense internal pressure from their repressions or superego, and can sometimes
suddenly kind of snap in various small ways and, under
enough pressure, behave in ways which might at first seem
totally out of sync with your view of them. I was not able
to see his eyes or facial expression; I was behind him on
the platform, partly because he walked more quickly in
general than I did—when I was a child, the term he used

for this was 'dawdle'—although, on that day, it was partly also because he and I were in the midst of yet another petty psychological struggle over the fact that I had overslept and made him, according to his perspective, 'late,' there being therefore something pointedly impatient about his rapid stride and hurry through the CTA station, to which I was responding by deliberately not increasing my own normal pace very much or making much of an effort to keep up with him, staying just far enough behind him to annoy him but not far enough back quite to warrant his turning and actually squeezing my shoes over it, as well as assuming a kind of spacey, apathetic demeanor—much like a dawdling child, in fact, though of course I would never have acknowledged this at the time. In other words, the basic situation was that he was peeved and I was sulking, but neither of us was consciously aware of this, nor of how habitual, for us, this sort of petty psychological struggle was—in retrospect, it seems to me that we did this sort of thing to one another constantly, out of possibly nothing more than unconscious habit. It's a typical sort of dynamic between fathers and sons. It may even have been part of the unconscious motivation behind my indifferent drifting and lump-like sloth at all of the various colleges he had to get up on time every day and go to work to pay for. Of course, none of this entered into my awareness at the time, much less ever got acknowledged or discussed by either of us. In some sense, you could say that my father died before either of us could become aware of how invested we actually were in these petty little rituals of conflict, or of how much it had affected their marriage that my mother had so often been put in the role of mediator between us, all of us acting out typical roles which none of us were conscious of, like machines going through their programmed motions.

I remember, hurrying through the platform's crowds, that I saw him turn sideways to shoulder his way between two large, slow-moving Hispanic women who were heading towards the train's open doors with twine-handled shopping bags, one of which my father's leg jostled and caused to swing slightly back and forth. I don't know whether these women were actually together or were just forced by their size and the surrounding crowds' pressure to walk so closely side by side. They were not among those interviewed after the accident, which means they were probably on the train by the time it happened. I was only eight to ten feet behind him by this time, and openly hurrying to catch up, as there was the idling downtown train just ahead, and the idea of my father just making it onto the train but of me lagging too far behind him and getting to the doors just as they closed, and of watching his face's expression framed by holly decals as we looked at one another through the doors' glass portions as he pulled away in the train—I think anyone could imagine how peeved and disgusted he would be, and also vindicated and triumphant in our little psychological struggle over hurry and 'lateness,' and I could now feel my own rising anxiety at the thought of him making the train and me just barely missing it, so at this point I was trying to close the gap between us. I still, to this day, do not know whether my father was aware then that I was almost right behind him, or that I was nearly butting and shoving people out of the way myself in my hurry to catch up, because, as far as I know, he did not look back over his shoulder or signal to me in any way as he made for the train's doors. During all of the litigation that followed, none of the respondents or their counsel ever once disputed the fact that CTA trains are not supposed to be able to begin moving unless all of the doors are completely closed. Nor did anyone seek to challenge my account of the exact order of what happened, as at this point I was a few feet at most behind him, and witnessed the whole thing with what everyone conceded was terrible clarity. The two halves of the car's door had begun to slide shut with their familiar pneumatic sound just as my father reached the doors and shot out one arm in between the halves to keep them from closing so that he could squeeze his way in, and the doors closed on his arm—too firmly, evidently, to allow either the rest of my father to squeeze through the doors' gap or to allow the doors to be forced back open enough to let him withdraw his arm, which it turned out was caused by a possible malfunction involving the machinery that controlled the force with which the doors closed—by which time the subway train had begun moving, which was another blatant malfunction—special circuit breakers between the doors' sensors and the train operator's console are supposed to disengage the throttle if any of the doors on any car are open (as one can imagine, we all learned a great deal about CTA trains' design and safety specifications during the litigation following the accident)—and my father was being forced to trot with gradually increasing speed alongside it, the train, releasing his hold on his head's hat to pound with his fist against the doors as two or possibly three men inside the subway car were now at the slight gap in the doors, trying to pull or pry them open further enough to at least allow my father to extract his arm. My father's hat, which he prized and owned a special hat block for, flew off and was lost in the platform's dense crowds, in which a visibly widening gap or tear appeared—by which I mean it appeared in the crowd further down the platform, which I could see from my own place, trapped in the crowd at the platform's edge at a point further and further behind the widening gap or fissure that opened in the platform's crowds as my father was forced to run faster and faster at the accelerating train's side and people moved or leapt back to avoid being knocked onto the track. Given that many of these people were also holding numerous small, subdivided packages and individually purchased bags, many of these could be seen flying up in the air and rotating or spilling their contents in various ways above the widening gap as shoppers jettisoned their purchases in an attempt to leap clear of my father's path, so that part of the appearance of the gap was the illusion that it was somehow spurting or raining consumer goods. Also, the causal issues related to legal liability for the incident turned out to be incredibly complex. The manufacturer's specifications for the doors' pneumatic systems did not adequately explain how the doors could close with such force that a healthy adult male could not withdraw his arm, which meant that the manufacturer's claim that my father—perhaps out of panic, or because of injury to his arm—failed to take reasonable action to extricate his arm was difficult to refute. The male subway riders who appeared to be attempting so forcefully to pry the doors open from within subsequently vanished down the track with the departing train and were not successfully identified, this due partly to the fact that the subsequent transit and police investigators did not pursue these identifications very aggressively, possibly as it was clear, even at the scene, that the incident was a civil and not criminal matter. My mother's first lawyer did place personal ads in the *Tribune* and *Sun-Times* requesting that these two or three passengers come forward and be deposed for legal purposes, but for what they claimed were reasons of expense and practicability, these ads were quite small, and were buried in the Classified section towards the rear of the paper, and ran for what my mother would later claim was an unreasonably brief and unaggressive period of time during which all too many Chicagoland residents left the city for the holidays anyhow—so that this eventually became one more protracted, complex element of the litigation's second phase.

At the Washington Square station, the official 'scene of the accident'—which, in a fatality, is legally deemed to be '[the] location at which death or injuries causing death are sustained'—was listed at 65 yards off of the subway platform, in the southbound tunnel itself, at which point the CTA train was determined to have been traveling at between 51 and 54 miles per hour and portions of my father's upper body impacted the iron bars of a built-in ladder protruding from the tunnel's west wall—this ladder had been installed to allow CTA maintenance personnel to access a box of multi-bus circuitry in the tunnel's ceiling— and the trauma, confusion, shock, noise, screaming, rain of small individual purchases, and nearly stampede-like evacuation of the platform as my father cut an increasingly forceful and high-velocity swath through the dense crowds of shoppers all disqualified even those few people who still remained there on the scene—most of them injured, or claiming injury—as 'reliable' witnesses for authorities to interview. Shock is evidently common in situations of graphic death. Less than an hour after the accident, all that any bystanders could seem to remember were screams, loss of holiday purchases, concern for personal safety, and vivid but fragmentary details as to my father's affect and actions, various rippling things the onrushing air did to his topcoat and scarf, and the successive injuries he appeared to receive as he was borne at increasing speed towards the platform's end and fully or partly collided with a wire mesh trash receptacle, several airborne packages and shopping bags, a pillar's steel rivets, and an older male commuter's steel or aluminum luggage cart—this last item was somehow knocked by the impact across the tunnel and onto the northbound tracks, causing sparks from that track's third rail and adding to the stampeding crowds' chaos. I remember that a young Hispanic or Puerto Rican man wearing what looked to be a type of tight black hairnet was interviewed while holding my father's right shoe, a tasseled Florsheim loafer, of which the toe portion and welt were so abraded by the platform's cement that the sole's front portion had detached and was hanging loose, and that the man could not recall how he'd come to be holding it. He, too, was later determined to be in shock, and I can clearly remember seeing the Hispanic man afterward again in the triage area of the emergency room—which was at Loyola Marymount Hospital, only one or two blocks away from the Washington Square CTA station—seated in a plastic chair and trying to fill out forms on a clipboard with a ballpoint pen attached by a piece of white string to the clipboard, still holding the shoe.

And the wrongful-death litigation was, as mentioned, incredibly complex, even though it all technically never even proceeded past the initial legal stages of determining whether the City of Chicago, the CTA, the CTA's Maintenance Division (the emergency brake's cord in the car to which my father was forcibly appended was discovered to have been vandalized and cut, although expert opinion was divided on whether the forensic evidence represented a very recent cut or one of weeks' duration. Evidently, the microscopic evaluation of severed plastic fibers can be interpreted in just about any way one's interests lead one to interpret it), the train's manufacturer of record, the train's engineer, his immediate supervisor, AFSCME, and the over two dozen different subcontractors and vendors of various components of the various systems adjudged by the forensic engineers retained by our legal team to have played a part in the accident should, as respondents, be classified in the action as strictly liable, liable, negligent, or FEDD, the latter abbreviation standing for 'failure to exercise due diligence.' According to my mother, our legal team's client liaison had confided to her that the multiplicity of named respondents was just an initial strategic gambit, and that we would ultimately be primarily suing the City of Chicago—which was, of course, my father's employer, in an ironic twist—citing 'common carrier tort law' and a precedent case entitled *Ybarra v. Coca-Cola* to justify collapsing liability onto the shoulders of the respondent that could be shown to have been most cheaply and efficiently able to take reasonable steps to prevent the accident—presumably by having required more stringent quality-assurance of the doors' pneumatics and sensors in the

CTA's contract with the train's manufacturer of record, a responsibility which fell, in a further irony, at least partly to the City of Chicago's bursar's office's cost systems division, in which one of my father's own responsibilities had involved weighted evaluations of up-front cost versus liability exposure in certain classes of city agencies' contracts—although fortunately, it turned out that CTA capital equipment expenditures were vetted by a different detail or team in cost systems. Anyhow, to my mother's, Joyce's, and my dismay, it became evident to us that our legal team's major criterion for arguing for different companies', agencies', and municipal entities' different liability designations involved those different possible respondents' cash resources and their respective insurance carriers' record of settlement in similar cases—that is, that the entire process was about numbers and money rather than anything like justice, responsibility, and the prevention of further wrongful, public, and totally undignified and pointless deaths. To be honest, I'm not sure that I'm explaining all this very well. As mentioned, the whole legal process was so complicated as to almost defy description, and the junior associate that the legal team had assigned to keep us apprised of developments and evolving strategies for the first sixteen months was not exactly the clearest or most empathetic counsel one could have hoped for. Plus it goes without saying that we were also all really upset, understandably, and my mother—whose emotional health had always been pretty delicate since the breakdown or abrupt changes of 1971–72 and subsequent divorce—was going in and out of what could probably be classified as disassociative shock or conversion reaction, and had actually moved back into the house in Libertyville that she'd shared with my father prior to their separation, supposedly ' just temporarily' and for reasons that changed each time Joyce or I pressed her on whether this moving back there was a very good idea for her, and she was generally not in good shape at all, psychologically speaking. In fact, after only the first round of depositions in an ancillary lawsuit between one of the respondents and its insurance company over just what percentage of the legal costs for the respondent's defense against our ongoing suit were covered in the respondent's liability policy with the insurance company—plus, to further complicate matters, a former partner in the lead law firm that was representing my mother and Joyce was now representing the insurance company, whose national headquarters turned out to be in Glenview, and there was a subsidiary set of briefs and depositions in that case concerning whether this fact could in any way constitute a conflict of interest—and procedurally, this ancillary suit had to be resolved or settled before preliminary depositions in our own suit—which by that point had evolved into the twin classifications of civil liability and wrongful death, and was so complex that it took almost a year for the team's litigators even to agree on how to file it correctly—such that, by this point, my mother's emotional state reached the point where she elected to discontinue all litigation, a decision which privately upset Joyce very much but which she, Joyce, was legally powerless to enjoin or influence, and there was then a very complicated domestic struggle in which Joyce kept trying, without my mother's knowledge, to get me to reinitiate the suit with myself, who was over twenty-one and the decedent's dependent and son, as sole plaintiff. But for complicated reasons—chief among them that I had been listed as a dependent on both my parents' 1977 federal tax returns, which, in my mother's case, would have been promptly disallowed in even a routine office audit, but which escaped notice in the more primitive Examinations environment of the Service in that era—it emerged that in order to do this, I would have had to have my mother declared legally 'non compos mentis,' which would have required a mandatory two-week psychiatric hospitalization for observation before we could obtain a legal declaration from a court-authorized psychiatrist, which was something no one in the family was even close to having the stomach for. So after sixteen months, the whole litigation process ended, with the exception of our former legal team's subsequent suit against my mother for recovery of fees and expenses that, to all appearances, the contract that Joyce and my mother signed had explicitly waived in lieu of a 40 percent contingency fee. The recondite arguments by which our former team was attempting to have this contract declared null and void because of some ambiguity in the legal language of one of their own contract's subclauses were never explained or made clear enough to me to be able to tell if they were anything more than frivolous or not, as at this juncture I was in my final semester at DePaul and also in the process of recruitment by the Service, and my mother and Joyce had to hire yet another lawyer to defend my mother against the former lawyers' suit, which still, if you can believe it, still drags on to this day, and is one of the main reasons my mother will give as a rationale for having become a virtual shut-in in the Libertyville house, where she still now resides, and for letting the home's telephone service lapse, although evidence of some kind of major psychological deterioration had already appeared much earlier, actually probably even in the midst of the original litigation and her moving back home to my father's house following the accident, with the first psychological symptom I can remember involving her growing preoccupation with the welfare of the birds in a nest of finches or starlings that for years had been up over one of the joists on the large, open wooden porch, which had been one of the chief attractions of the Libertyville house when my parents had made the original decision to move there, the obsession then progressing from that one nest to the neighborhood's birds in general, and she began having more and more standing and tube-style feeders installed on the porch and the front lawn and buying and leaving out more and more seed and then eventually also all different kinds of human food and various 'bird supplies' for them on the steps of the porch, at one low point including tiny pieces of furniture from a dollhouse from her girlhood in Beloit, which I knew she had treasured as memorabilia as I'd heard her recount all sorts of childhood anecdotes to Joyce about how much she'd treasured the thing and had collected miniature furniture for it, and which she'd kept for many years in the storage room of the Libertyville house, along with a lot of memorabilia from my own early childhood in Rockford, and Joyce, who has remained my mother's loyal friend and sometimes virtual nurse—even though she did, in 1979, fall head over heels in love with the attorney who helped them close Speculum Books under Chapter 13 provisions, and is now married to him and lives with him and his two children in

Wilmette—Joyce agrees that the tedious, complex, cynical endlessness of the accident's legal fallout was a large part of what kept my mother from processing the trauma of my father's passing and working through some of the prior, 1971-era unresolved emotions and conflicts which the accident had now brought rushing back up to the surface. Although at a certain point you have to just suck it up and play the hand you're dealt and get on with your life, in my own opinion.

But I remember once, during an afternoon on which he'd paid me to help him with some light yard work, asking my father why he never seemed to dispense direct advice about life the way my friends' fathers did. At the time, his failure to give advice seemed to me to be evidence that he was either unusually taciturn and repressed, or else that he just didn't care enough. In hindsight, I now realize that the reason was not the former and never the second, but rather that my father was, in his own particular way, somewhat wise, at least about certain things. In this instance, he was wise enough to be suspicious of his own desire to seem wise, and to refuse to indulge it—this could make him seem aloof and uncaring, but what he really was was disciplined. He was an adult; he had himself firmly in hand. This remains largely theory, but my best guess as to his never dispensing wisdom like other dads is that my father understood that advice—even wise advice—actually does nothing for the advisee, changes nothing inside, and can actually cause confusion when the advisee is made to feel the wide gap between the comparative simplicity of the advice and the totally muddled complication of his own situation and path. I'm not putting this very well. If you begin to get the idea that other people can actually *live* by the clear, simple principles of good advice, it can make you feel even worse about your own inabilities. It can cause self-pity, which I think my father recognized as the great enemy of life and contributor to nihilism. Although it's not as though he and I talked about it in any depth—that would have been too much like advice. I can't remember how he specifically answered that day's question. I remember asking it, including where we stood and how the rake felt in my hands as I asked it, but then there's a blank after that. My best guess, derived from my knowledge of our dynamics, would be that he would say trying to advise me about what to do or not do would be like the childhood fable's rabbit 'begging' not to be thrown in the briar patch. Whose name escapes me, though. But obviously meaning he felt it would have the reverse effect. He might have even laughed in a dry way, as though the question was comical in its lack of awareness of our dynamics and the obvious answer. It would probably be the same if I had asked him if he believed I didn't respect him or his advice. He might act as if he was amused that I was so unaware of myself, that I was incapable of respect but didn't even know it. It is, as mentioned, possible that he simply didn't like me very much, and that he used a dry, sophisticated wittiness to sort of try to deal with that fact within himself. It would, I imagine, be hard on someone not to be able to like your own offspring. There would obviously be some guilt involved. I know that even the slumped, boneless way I sat when watching TV or listening to music peeved him—not directly, but it was another thing I used to overhear him speaking about in arguments with my mother. For what it's worth, I accept the basic idea that parents instinctively do 'love' their offspring no matter what—the evolutionary reasoning behind this premise is too obvious to ignore. But actually 'liking' them, or enjoying them as people, seems like a totally different thing. It may be that psychologists are off-base in their preoccupation with children's need to feel that their father or some other parent loves them. It also seems valid to consider the child's desire to feel that a parent actually likes them, as love itself is so automatic and preprogrammed in a parent that it isn't a very good test of whatever it is that the typical child feels so anxious to pass the test of. It's not unlike the religious confidence that one is 'loved unconditionally' by God—as the God in question is defined as something that loves this way automatically and universally, it doesn't seem to really have anything to do with you, so it's hard to see why religious people claim to feel such reassurance in being loved this way by God. The point here is not that every last feeling and emotion must be taken personally as about you, but only that, for basic psychological reasons, it's difficult not to feel this way when it comes to one's father—it's simply human nature.

Anyhow, all this is part of the question of how I came to be posted here in Examinations—the unexpected coincidences, changes in priorities and direction. Obviously, these sorts of unexpected things can happen in all sorts of different ways, and it's dangerous to make too much of them. I remember having one roommate—this was at Lindenhurst College—who was a self-professed Christian. I actually had two roommates in the Lindenhurst dorm suite, with a shared communal 'social room' in the center and three small single bedrooms leading off of it, which was an excellent rooming setup—but one of these room-mates in particular was a Christian, as was his girlfriend. Lindenhurst, which was the first college I attended, was a peculiar place in that it was primarily a school full of Chicagoland-area hippies and wastoids, but also had a fervent Christian minority who were totally separate from the overall life of the school. *Christian* in this case mean-ing evangelical, just like Jimmy Carter's sister, who, if I remember it correctly, was reported as going around per-forming freelance exorcisms. The fact that members of this evangelical branch of Protestantism refer to themselves as just 'Christians,' as though there were only one real kind, is usually enough to characterize them, at least as far as I was concerned. This one had come in via the suite's third roommate, whom I knew and liked, and who arranged the whole three-way rooming situation without me or the Christian ever meeting one another until it was too late. The Christian was definitely not anyone I would have gone out and recruited to room with on my own, although in fairness, he didn't much care for my lifestyle or what room-ing with me involved, either. The arrangement ended up being highly temporary, anyhow. I remember that he was from upstate Indiana, was fervently involved in a college organization called Campus Crusade, and had numerous pairs of dress chinos and blue blazers and Topsiders, and a smile that looked as though someone had plugged him in. He also had an equally evangelical Christian girlfriend or platonic female friend who would come over a great deal— she practically lived there, from what I could see—and I have a clear, detailed memory of one incident when the three of us were all in the communal area, which in these dormitories' nomenclature was called the 'social room,' but in which I often liked to sit on the third roommate's soft old vinyl sofa alone instead of in my tiny bedroom, to read, double on Obetrol, or sometimes smoke my little brass one-hitter and watch TV, prompting all sorts of predictable arguments with the Christian, who often liked to treat the social room as a Christian clubhouse and have his girlfriend and all his other high-wattage Christian friends in to drink Fresca and fellowship about Campus Crusade matters or the fulfillment of apocalyptic prophecy, and so on and so forth, and liked to squeeze my shoes and remind me that it was called 'the social room' when I asked them all whether they didn't have some frightening pamphlets to get out of there and go distribute somewhere or something. In hindsight, it seems obvious that I actually liked despising the Christian because I could pretend that the evangelicals' smugness and self-righteousness were the only real antithesis or alternative to the cynical, nihilistically wastoid attitude I was starting to cultivate in myself. As if there was nothing in between these two extremes—which, ironically, was exactly what the evangelical Christians also believed. Meaning I was much more like the Christian than either of us would ever be willing to admit. Of course, at barely nineteen, I was totally unaware of all this. At the time, all I knew is that I despised the Christian and enjoyed calling him 'Pepsodent Boy' and complaining about him to the third roommate, who was in a rock band besides his classes and was usually not around the suite very much, leaving the Christian and me to mock and bait and judge and use one another to confirm our respective smug prejudices.

Anyhow, at one juncture, I, the Christian roommate, and his girlfriend—who might technically have been his fiancée—were all sitting around in the suite's social room, and for some reason—quite possibly unprompted—the girlfriend was seeing fit to tell me the story of how she was 'saved' or 'born again' and became a Christian. I remember almost nothing about her except for the fact that she wore pointy-toed leather cowboy boots decorated with flowers—that is, not cartoons of flowers or isolated floral designs but a rich, detailed, photorealist scene of some kind of meadow or garden in full bloom, so that the boots looked more like a calendar or greeting card. Her testimony, as best as I can now recall, was set on a certain day an unspecified amount of time before, a day when she said she was feeling totally desolate and lost and nearly at the end of her rope, sort of wandering aimlessly in the psychological desert of our younger generation's decadence and materialism and so on and so forth. Fervent Christians are always remembering themselves as—and thus, by extension, judging everyone else outside their sect to be—lost and hopeless and just barely clinging to any kind of interior sense of value or reason to even go on living, before they were 'saved.' And that she happened, on this one day, to be driving along a county road outside her hometown, just wandering, driving aimlessly around in one of her parents' AMC Pacer, until, for no particular reason she was aware of inside herself, she turned suddenly into the parking lot of what turned out to be an evangelical Christian church, which by coincidence happened to be right in the middle of holding an evangelical service, and—for what she again claimed was no discernible reason or motive she could have named—she wandered aimlessly in and sat down in the rear of the church in one of the plushly cushioned theater-type seats their churches tend to use instead of wooden pews, and just as she sat down, the preacher or father or whatever they called them there evidently said, 'There is someone out there with us in the congregation today that is feeling lost and hopeless and at the end of their rope and needs to know that Jesus loves them very, very much,' and then—in the social room, recounting her story—the girl-friend testified as to how she had been stunned and deeply moved, and said she had instantly felt a huge, dramatic spiritual change deep inside of her in which she said she felt completely reassured and unconditionally known and loved, and as though now suddenly her life had meaning and direction to it after all, and so on and so forth, and that furthermore she had not had a down or empty moment since, not since the pastor or father or whatever picked just that moment to reach out past all the other evangelical Christians sitting there fanning themselves with complimentary fans with slick full-color ads for the church on them and to just kind of verbally nudge them aside out of the way and somehow address himself directly to the girl-friend and her circumstances at just that moment of deep spiritual need. She talked about herself as though she were a car whose pistons had been pulled and valves ground. In hindsight, of course, there turned out to be certain parallels with my own case, but the only real response I had at the time was that I felt annoyed—they both always annoyed the hell out of me, and I can't remember what I could have been doing that day sitting there in conversation with them, the circumstances—and I can remember making

a show of having my tongue pressing against the inside
of my cheek in such a way as to produce a visible bulge
in my cheek and giving the girlfriend in the boots a dry,
sardonic look, and asking her just what exactly had made
her think the evangelical pastor was talking to her directly,
meaning her in particular, as probably everyone else sitting
there in the church audience probably felt the same way
she did, as pretty much every red-blooded American in
today's (then) late-Vietnam and Watergate era felt desolate and disillusioned and unmotivated and directionless
and lost, and that what if the preacher or father's saying
'Someone here's lost and hopeless' was tantamount to those
Sun-Times horoscopes that are specially designed to be so
universally obvious that they always give their horoscope
readers (like Joyce every morning, over vegetable juice she
made herself in a special machine) that special eerie feeling
of particularity and insight, exploiting the psychological
fact that most people are narcissistic and prone to the illusion that they and their problems are uniquely special and
that if they're feeling a certain way then surely they're the
only person who is feeling like that. In other words, I was
only pretending to ask her a question—I was actually giving the girlfriend a condescending little lecture on people's
narcissism and illusion of uniqueness, like the fat indus-
trialist in Dickens or *Ragged Dick* who leans back from a
giant dinner with his fingers laced over his huge stomach
and cannot imagine how anyone in that moment could be
hungry anywhere in the whole world. I also remember that
the Christian's girlfriend was a large, copper-haired girl
with something slightly wrong with one of the teeth on
either side of her front teeth, which overlapped one of the

front teeth in a distracting way, because during that day's conversation she gave me a big smug smile and said that, why, she didn't think that my cynical comparison was any kind of refutation or nullification of her vital Christ experience that day or its effect on her inner rebirth at all, not one little bit. She may have looked over at the Christian for reassurance or an 'Amen' or something at this juncture—I can't remember what the Christian was doing all through this exchange. I do, though, remember giving her a big, exaggerated smile right back and saying, 'Whatever,' and thinking inwardly she wasn't worth wasting time arguing with, and what was I even doing here talking to them, and that she and Pepsodent Boy deserved one another—and I know sometime soon after that I left them together in the social room and went off while thinking about the whole conversation and feeling somewhat lost and desolate inside, but also consoled that I was at least superior to narcissistic rubes like these two so-called Christians. And then I have a slightly later memory of me standing at a party with a red plastic cup of beer and telling somebody the story of the interchange in such a way that I appeared smart and funny and the girlfriend was a total fool. I know I was nearly always the hero of any story or incident I ever told people about during this period—which, like the thing with the lone sideburn, is a memory that makes me almost wince now.

Anyhow, it seems like a very long time ago. But the point of even remembering the conversation, I think, is that there was an important fact behind the Christian girl's 'salvation' story which I simply hadn't understood at the time—and, to be honest, I don't think she or the

Christian did, either. It's true that her story was stupid
and dishonest, but that doesn't mean the experience she
had in the church that day didn't happen, or that its
effects on her weren't real. I'm not putting it very well, but
I was both right and wrong about her little story. I think
the truth is probably that enormous, sudden, dramatic,
unexpected, life-changing experiences are not translatable
or explainable to anyone else, and this is because they
really *are* unique and particular—though not unique in
the way the Christian girl believed. This is because their
power isn't just a result of the experience itself, but also
of the circumstances in which it hits you, of everything
in your previous life-experience which has led up to it
and made you exactly who and what you are when the
experience hits you. Does that make any sense? It's hard
to explain. What the girl with the meadow on her boots
had left out of the story was why she was feeling so especially desolate and lost right then, and thus why she was
so psychologically 'primed' to hear the pastor's general,
anonymous comment in that personal way. To be fair,
maybe she couldn't remember why. But still, all she really
told was her little story's dramatic climax, which was
the preacher's comment and the sudden inward changes
she felt as a result, which is a little like telling just the
punch line of a joke and expecting the person to laugh. As
Chris Acquistipace would put it, her story was just data;
there was no fact-pattern. On the other hand, it's always
possible that the 25,834 words so far of my own life-
experience won't seem relevant or make sense to anyone
but me—which would make this not unlike the Christian
girl's own attempt to explain how she got to where she

was, assuming she was even sincere about the dramatic changes inside. It's easy to delude yourself, obviously.

Anyhow, as mentioned, a crucial element in my entering the Service was ending up in the wrong but identical classroom at DePaul in December 1978, which I was so immersed in staying focused for the *Federalist Papers* review that I didn't even notice my error until the prof walked in. I couldn't tell whether he was the real fearful Jesuit or not. I only later found out that he wasn't the Advanced Tax instructor of record—there had evidently been some sort of personal emergency for the course's regular Jesuit prof, and this one had taken over as a sub for the last two weeks. Hence the initial confusion. I remember thinking that, for a Jesuit, the prof was in definite 'mufti.' He wore an archaically conservative dark-gray suit whose boxy look might have been actual flannel, and his dress shoes' shine was dazzling when the classroom's overhead fluorescents hit them at the proper angle. He seemed lithe and precise; his movements had the brisk economy of a man who knows time is a valuable asset. In terms of realizing my mistake, this was also when I stopped mentally reviewing the *Federalist* and became aware of a markedly different vibe among the students in this classroom. Several wore neckties under sweater vests, a couple of these vests being actual argyle. Every last shoe I could see was a black or brown leather business shoe, their laces neatly tied. To this day, I do not know precisely how I took the wrong building's door. I am not the sort of person who gets lost easily, and I knew Garnier Hall, as it's where the Intro Accounting class also met. Anyhow, to reiterate, on this day I had somehow gone to 311 Garnier Hall, instead of my own political science class's identical 311 Daniel Hall directly across the transom, and had sat down along the side wall near the room's extreme rear, a spot from which, once I came out of my preoccupation and realized my error, I would have had to cause a lot of disruption and moving of book bags and down jackets in order to get out—the room was completely filled by the time the substitute came in. Later, I learned that a few of the room's most obviously serious and adult-looking students, with actual briefcases and accordion files instead of backpacks, were graduate students in DePaul's advanced-degree business program—the Advanced Tax course was that advanced. Actually, DePaul's whole accounting department was very serious and strong—accounting and business administration were institutional strengths that DePaul was known for and spent a good deal of time extolling in its brochures and promotional materials. Obviously, this isn't why I had reenrolled at DePaul—I had next to no interest in accounting except, as mentioned, to prove something or compensate my father by finally passing Intro. The school's accounting program turned out to be so high-powered and respected, though, that nearly half of that classroom's Advanced Tax students were already signed up to take the February 1979 CPA exam, although at that time I barely knew what this licensing exam even was, or that it took several months of study and practice to prepare for. For instance, I learned later that the final exam in Advanced Tax was actually designed to be a microcosm of some of the taxation sections of the CPA exam. My father, by the way, also held a CPA license, though he rarely used it in his job with the city. In hindsight, though, and in the light of all that eventuated from that day, I'm not even sure I would have walked out even if the logistics of leaving hadn't been so awkward—not once the substitute came in. Even though I really did need that final-exam review in American Political Thought, I still may have stayed. I'm not sure I can explain it. I remember he came briskly in and hung his topcoat and hat on a hook on the corner's flag-stand. To this day, I can never be totally sure whether bumbling into the wrong building's 311 right before final exams might not just have been one more bit of unconscious irresponsibility on my part. You cannot analyze sudden, dramatic experiences like this this way, though—especially in hindsight, which is notoriously tricky (though I obviously did not understand this during the exchange with the Christian girl in the boots).

At the time, I did not know how old the substitute was—as mentioned, I only learned later that he was filling in for the class's real Jesuit father, whose absence seemed unmourned—or even his name. My main experience with substitutes had been in high school. In terms of age, all I knew was that he was in that amorphous (to me) area between forty and sixty. I don't know how to describe him, though he made an immediate impression. He was slender, and in the room's bright lighting he looked pale in a way that seemed luminous instead of sickly, and had a steel-colored crew cut and a sort of pronounced facial bone structure. Overall, he looked to me like someone in an archaic photo or daguerreotype. His business suit's trousers were double pleated, which added to the impression of box-like solidity. Also, he had good posture, which my father always referred to as a person's 'carriage'—upright and square-shouldered without seeming stiff—and as he came briskly in with his accordion file filled with neatly organized and labeled course materials, all of the room's accounting students seemed unconsciously to shift and sit up a little straighter at their little desks. He pulled down the A/V screen before the board much as one would pull down a window's shade, using his pocket handkerchief to touch the screen's handle. To the best of my recollection, nearly everyone in the room was male. A handful were also oriental. He was getting his materials out and arranging them, looking down at his desktop with a little formal smile. What he was actually doing was the teacherly thing of acknowledging the roomful of students without looking at them. They in turn were totally focused, to a man. The whole room was different from political science or psychology classes, or even Intro Accounting, where there was always litter on the floor and people slouched back on their tailbones in their seats and looked openly up at the clock or yawned, and there was always a constant restless, whispery undertone which the Intro Accounting professor pretended wasn't there—maybe the normal profs no longer even heard the sound, or were immune to students' open displays of tedium and inattention. When the substitute accounting professor entered, however, this room's whole voltage changed. I don't know how to describe it. Nor can I totally rationally explain why I stayed—which, as mentioned, meant missing the final review in American Political Thought. At the time, continuing to sit there in the wrong class seemed like just one more feckless, undisciplined impulse. Maybe I was embarrassed to have the sub see me leave. Unlike the Christian girlfriend, I never seem to recognize important moments at the time they're going on—they always seem like distractions from what I'm really supposed to be doing. One way to explain it is that there was just something about him—the substitute. His expression had the same burnt, hollow concentration of photos of military veterans who'd been in some kind of real war, meaning combat. His eyes held us whole, as a group. I know I suddenly felt uncomfortable about my painter's pants and untied Timberlands, but if the substitute reacted to them one way or the other, he gave no sign. When he signified the official start of class by looking at his watch, it was with a crisp gesture of bringing his wrist sharply out and around, like a boxer's left cross, the force pulling up the sleeve of his suit jacket slightly to disclose a stainless steel Piaget, which I remember at the time struck me as a surprisingly racy watch for a Jesuit.

He used the white A/V screen for transparencies—unlike the Intro prof, he didn't write things in chalk on the blackboard—and when he put the first transparency on the overhead projector and the room's lights dimmed, his face was lit from below like a cabaret performer's, which made its hollow intensity and facial structure even more pronounced. I remember there was a sort of electric coolness in my head. The diagram projected behind him was an upward curve with bar graphs extending below its various sections, the curve steep near the origin and flattening somewhat at the apex. It looked a bit like a wave preparing to break. The diagram was unlabeled, and only later would I recognize it as representing the progressive marginal rate schedules for the 1976 federal income tax. I felt unusually aware and alert, but in a different way from doubling or Cylert. There were also several curves and equations and glossed citations from USTC §62, many of whose subsections had to do with complex regulations about the distinction between deductions 'for' adjusted gross income versus deductions 'from' AGI, which the substitute said formed the basis of practically every truly effective modern individual tax-planning strategy. Here—though I realized this only later, after recruitment—he was referring to structuring one's affairs so that as many deductions as possible were deductions 'for' adjusted gross income, as everything from the Standard Deduction to medical-expense deductions are designed with AGI-based floors (*floor* meaning, for example, that as only those medical expenses in excess of 3 percent of AGI were deductible, it was obviously to the advantage of the average taxpayer to render his AGI—known also sometimes as his '31,' as it was then on Line 31 of the Individual 1040 that one entered AGI—just as low as possible).

Admittedly, though, however alert and aware I felt, I was probably more aware of the effects the lecture seemed to be having on me than of the lecture itself, much of which was over my head—understandably, as I hadn't even finished Intro Accounting yet—and yet was almost impossible to look away from or not feel stirred by. This was partly due to the substitute's presentation, which was rapid, organized, undramatic, and dry in the way of people who know that what they are saying is too valuable in its own right to cheapen with concern about delivery or 'connecting' with the students. In other words, the presentation had a kind of zealous integrity that manifested not as style but as the lack of it. I felt that I suddenly, for the first time, understood the meaning of my father's term 'no-nonsense,' and why it was a term of approval.

I remember I did notice that the class's students all took notes, which in accounting classes means that one has to internalize and write down one fact or point from the professor while at the same time still listening intently enough to the next point to be able to write it down next, as well, which requires a kind of intensively split concentration that I did not get the hang of until well into T&A in Indianapolis the following year. It was a totally different type of note-taking from the kind in humanities classes, which involved mainly doodles and broad, abstract themes and ideas. Also, the Advanced Tax students had multiple pencils lined up on their desks, all of which were extremely sharp. I realized that I almost never had a sharp pencil at hand when I really wanted one; I had never taken the trouble to keep them organized and sharpened. The only touch of what might have been dry wit in the lecture was occasional statements and quotes that the substitute interpolated into the graphs by sometimes writing them on the current transparency, projecting them onto the A/V screen without comment and then pausing while everyone copied them all down as quickly as possible before he changed to the next transparency. I still remember one such example—'What we now need to discover in the social realm is the moral equivalent of war,' with the only written attribution at the end being 'James,' which, at the time, I believed referred to the biblical apostle James, for obvious reasons—although he said nothing to explain or reinforce the quote while the six straight rows of students—some of whose glasses reflected the projection's light in ways that gave them an openly robotic, conformist aspect, with twin squares of white light where their eyes should have been, I remember being struck by—dutifully transcribed it. Or one other example, which was preprinted on its own transparency and credited to Karl Marx, the well-known father of Marxism—

> 'In Communist society it will be possible for me to do one thing today and another tomorrow, to hunt in the morning, fish in the afternoon, rear cattle in the evening, criticize after dinner, <u>just as I please</u>'—

about which the substitute's only gloss was the dry statement 'Emphasis added.'

What I'm trying to say is that it was ultimately much more like the evangelist girlfriend with the boots' own experience than I could have ever admitted at the time. Obviously, through just the 2,235-word story of a memory, I could never convince anybody else that the innate, objective quality of the substitute's lecture would also have glued anybody else to their seat and made them forget about their final review in American Political Thought, or of the way that much of what the Catholic father (I thought) said or projected seemed somehow aimed directly at me. I can, though, at least help explain why I was so 'primed' for experiencing it this way, as I'd already had a kind of foretaste or temblor of just this experience shortly before the mistake in final-review classes' rooms occurred, though it was only later, in retrospect, that I understood it—meaning the experience—as such.

I can clearly remember that a few days earlier—meaning on the Monday of the last week of regular classes for the Fall '78 term—I was sitting there all slumped and unmotivated on the old yellow corduroy couch in our DePaul dorm room in the middle of the afternoon. I was by myself, wearing nylon warm-up pants and a black Pink Floyd tee shirt, trying to spin a soccer ball on my finger, and watching the CBS soap opera *As the World Turns* on the room's little black-and-white Zenith—not Obetrolling or blowing off anything in particular but essentially still just being an unmotivated lump. There was certainly always reading and studying for finals I could do, but I was being a wastoid. I was slouched way down on my tail-bone on the couch, so that everything on the little TV was framed by my knees, and watching *As the World Turns* while spinning the soccer ball in an idle, undirected way. It was technically the roommate's television, but he was a serious pre-med student and always at the science library, though he had taken the trouble to rig a specially folded wire coat hanger to take the place of the Zenith's missing antenna, which was the only reason it got any reception at all. *As the World Turns* ran on CBS from 1:00 to 2:00 in the afternoon. This was something I still did too much during that final year, sitting there wasting time in front of the little Zenith, and several times I'd gotten passively sucked into CBS afternoon soap operas, where the shows' characters all spoke and emoted broadly and talked to one another without any hitch or pause in intensity whatsoever, it seemed, so that there was something almost hypnotic about the whole thing, especially as I had no classes on Monday or Friday and it was all too easy to sit there and get sucked in. I can remember that many of the other DePaul students that year were hooked on the ABC soap opera

General Hospital, gathering in great avid, hooting packs to watch it—with their hip alibi being that they were actually making fun of the show—but, for reasons that probably had to do with the Zenith's spotty reception, I was more of a CBS habitué that year, particularly *As the World Turns* and *Guiding Light,* which followed *As the World Turns* at 2:00 P.M. on weekdays and was actually in some ways an even more hypnotic show.

Anyhow, I was sitting there trying to spin the ball on my finger and watching the soap opera, which was also heavily loaded with commercials—especially in the second half, which soap operas tend to load with more commercials, as they figure that you're already sucked in and mesmerized and will sit still for more ads—and at the end of every commercial break, the show's trademark shot of planet earth as seen from space, turning, would appear, and the CBS daytime network announcer's voice would say, '*You're watching* As the World Turns,' which he seemed, on this particular day, to say more and more pointedly each time—'*You're watching* As the World Turns,' until the tone began to seem almost incredulous—'*You're watching* As the World Turns'—until I was suddenly struck by the bare reality of the statement. I don't mean any sort of humanities-type ironic metaphor, but the literal thing he was saying, the simple surface level. I don't know how many times I'd heard this that year while sitting around watching *As the World Turns,* but I suddenly realized that the announcer was actually saying over and over what I was literally doing. Not only this, but I also realized that I had been told this fact countless times—as I said, the announcer's statement followed every commercial break after each segment of the show—without ever being even slightly aware of the literal reality of what I was doing. I was not Obetrolling at this moment of awareness, I should add. This was different. It was as if the CBS announcer were speaking directly to me, shaking my shoulder or leg as though trying to arouse someone from sleep—'*You're watching* As the World Turns.' It's hard to explain. It was not even the obvious double entendre that struck me. This was more literal, which somehow had made it harder to see. All of this hit me, sitting there. It could not have felt more concrete if the announcer had actually said, '*You are sitting on an old yellow dorm couch, spinning a black-and-white soccer ball, and watching* As the World Turns, *without ever even acknowledging to yourself this is what you are doing.*' This is what struck me. It was beyond being feckless or a wastoid—it's like I wasn't even there. The truth is I was not even aware of the obvious double entendre of '*You're watching* As the World Turns' until three days later—the show's almost terrifying pun about the passive waste of time of sitting there watching something whose reception through the hanger didn't even come in very well, while all the while real things in the world were going on and people with direction and initiative were taking care of business in a brisk, no-nonsense way—meaning not until Thursday morning, when this secondary meaning suddenly struck me in the middle of taking a shower before getting dressed and hurrying to what I intended—consciously, at any rate—to be the final-exam review in American Political Thought. Which may have been one reason why I was so preoccupied and took the wrong building's entrance, I suppose. At the time, though, on Monday afternoon, all that hit home with me was the reiteration of the simple fact of what I was doing, which was, of course, nothing, just slumped there like something without any bones, uninvolved even in the surface reality of watching Victor deny his paternity to Jeanette (even though Jeanette's son has the same extremely rare genetic blood disorder that's kept putting Victor in the hospital throughout much of the semester. Victor may in some sense have actually 'believed' his own denials, I remember thinking, as he essentially seemed like that kind of person) between my knees.

But nor is it as though I consciously reflected on all of this at the time. At the time, I was aware only of the concrete impact of the announcer's statement, and the dawning realization that all of the directionless drifting and laziness and being a 'wastoid' which so many of us in that era pretended to have raised to a nihilistic art form, and believed was cool and funny (I too had thought it was cool, or at least I believed I thought so—there had seemed to be something almost romantic about flagrant waste and drifting, which Jimmy Carter was ridiculed for calling 'malaise' and telling the nation to snap out of it) was, in reality, not funny, not one bit funny, but rather frightening, in fact, or sad, or something else—something I could not name because it has no name. I knew, sitting there, that I might be a real nihilist, that it wasn't always just a hip pose. That I drifted and quit because nothing meant anything, no one choice was really better. That I was, in a way, too free, or that this kind of freedom wasn't actually real—I was free to choose 'whatever' because it didn't really matter. But that this, too, was because of something I chose—I had somehow chosen to have nothing matter. It all felt much less abstract than it sounds to try to explain it. All this was happening while I was just sitting there, spinning the ball. The point was that, through making this choice, I didn't matter, either. I didn't stand for anything. If I wanted to matter—even just to myself—I would have to be less free, by deciding to choose in some kind of definite way. Even if it was nothing more than an act of will. All of these awarenesses were very rapid and indistinct, and the realizations about choosing and mattering were as far as I got—I was also still trying to watch *As the World Turns,* which tended to get steadily more dramatic and compelling as it progressed towards the hour's end, as they always wanted to make you remember to tune in again the next day. But the point was that I realized, on some level, that whatever a potentially 'lost soul' was, I was one—and it wasn't cool or funny. And, as mentioned, it was only a few days later that I mistakenly ended up across the transom in the final-class session of Advanced Tax—which was, I should stress, a subject which at that time I had zero interest in, I believed. Like most people outside the industry, I imagined tax accountancy to be the province of fussy little men with thick glasses and elaborate stamp collections, more or less the opposite of hip or cool—and the experience of hearing the CBS announcer spell out surface reality over and over, of suddenly really being aware of hearing him, and of seeing the little screen between my knees, beneath the spinning ball on my finger's point was part of what put me in a position, I think, whether mistakenly or not, to hear something that changed my direction.

I remember that the third-floor's hallway's bell had rung at the end of the scheduled time for Advanced Tax that day without any of the students doing that end-of-class thing in humanities classes of fidgeting around to gather their materials together or leaning over their desks to retrieve their bags and briefcases from the floor, even as the substitute turned off the overhead projector and raised the A/V screen with a smart snap of his left hand, replacing the handkerchief in his suit coat's pocket. They all remained quiet and attentive. As the room's overhead lights came back on, I remember glancing and seeing that the older, mustachioed student beside me's class notes were almost unbelievably neat and well-organized, with Roman numerals for the lecture's main points and lowercase letters, inset numbers, and double indents for subheadings and corollaries. His handwriting itself looked almost automated, it was that good. This was despite the fact that they were essentially written in the dark. Several digital watches beeped the hour in sync. Just like its mirror opposite across the transom, Garnier 311's floor was tiled in an institutional tan-and-brown pattern that was either checkerboard or interlocking diamonds, depending on one's angle or perspective. All of this I remember very clearly.

Though it would be over a year before I understood them, here are just a few of the substitute's review lecture's main areas, as denumerated in the older business student's notes:

Imputed Income→Haig-Simons Formula
Constructive Receipt
Limited Partnerships, Passive Losses
Amortization and Capitalization→1976 TRA §266
Depreciation→Class Life System

Cash Method v. Accrual Method → Implications
for AGI
Inter vivos Gifts and 76 TRA
Straddle Techniques
4 Criteria for Nontaxable Exchange
Client Tax Planning Strategy ('Tailoring
the Transaction') v. IRS Exams Strategy
('Collapsing the Transaction')

It was, as mentioned, the final regular class day of the term. The end of the final regular class, in the humanities courses I was used to taking, was usually the moment for the younger professor to try to make some kind of hip, self-mocking summation—*'Mr. Gorton, would you briefly summarize what we've learned over the past sixteen weeks, please?'*—as well as instructions about the logistics of the final exam or paper, and final grades, and perhaps wishes for a good holiday recess (it was two weeks before Christmas 1978). In Advanced Tax, though, when the substitute turned from raising the screen, he gave none of the bodily signals of completion or transition to final instructions or summary. He stood very still—noticeably stiller than most people stand when they stand still. Thus far, he had spoken 8,206 words, counting numeric terms and operators. The older males and Asians all still sat there, and it seemed that this instructor was able to make eye contact with all forty-eight of us at once. I was aware that part of this substitute's vibe of dry, aloof, effortless authority was due to the way the class's upperclassmen all paid such attention to his every word and gesture. It was obvious that they respected this substitute, and that it was a respect that he didn't have to return, or feign returning, in order to accept. He was not anxious to 'connect' or be liked. But nor was he hostile or patronizing. What he seemed to be was 'indifferent'—not in a meaningless, drifting, nihilistic way, but rather in a secure, self-confident way. It's hard to describe, although I remember the awareness of it very clearly. The word that kept arising in my mind as he looked at us and we all watched and waited—although all of this took place very quickly—was *credibility*, as in the phrase 'credibility gap' from the Watergate scandal, which had essentially been going on while I was at Lindenhurst. The sounds of other accounting, economics, and business administration classes emptying into the hallway were ignored. Instead of gathering together his materials, the substitute—who, as mentioned, I thought at the time was a Jesuit father in 'mufti'—had put his hands behind his back and paused, looking at us. The whites of his eyes were extremely white, the way usually only a dark complexion can make eyes' whites look. I've forgotten the irises' color. His complexion, though, was that of someone who had rarely been out in the sun. He seemed at home in thrifty, institutional fluorescent light. His bow tie was perfectly straight and flush even though it was the hand-tied kind, not a clip-on.

He said, 'You will want something of a summation, then. An hortation.' (It is not impossible that I misheard him and what he actually said was 'exhortation.') He looked quickly at his watch, making the same right-angled movement. 'All right,' he said. A small smile played around his mouth as he said 'All right,' but it was clear that he wasn't joking or trying to slightly undercut what he was about to say, the way so many humanities profs of that era

tended to mock themselves or their hortations in order
to avoid seeming uncool. It only struck me later, after I'd
entered the Service's TAC, that this substitute was actually
the first instructor I'd seen at any of the schools I'd drifted
in and out of who seemed a hundred percent indifferent
about being liked or seen as cool or likable by the students,
and realized—I did, once I'd entered the Service—what
a powerful quality this sort of indifference could be in an
authority figure. Actually, in hindsight, the substitute may
have been the first genuine authority figure I ever met,
meaning a figure with genuine 'authority' instead of just
the power to judge you or squeeze your shoes from their
side of the generation gap, and I became aware for the
first time that 'authority' was actually something real and
authentic, that a real authority was not the same as a friend
or someone who cared about you, but nevertheless could
be good for you, and that the authority relation was not a
'democratic' or equal one and yet could have value for both
sides, both people in the relation. I don't think I'm explaining this very well—but it's true that I did feel singled out,
spindled on those eyes in a way I neither liked nor didn't,
but was certainly aware of. It was a certain kind of power
that he exerted and that I was granting him, voluntarily.
That respect was not the same as coercion, although it was
a kind of power. It was all very strange. I also noticed that
now he had his hands behind his back, in something like
the 'parade rest' military position.

He said to the accounting students, 'All right, then.
Before you leave here to resume that crude approximation of a human life you have heretofore called a life, I
will undertake to inform you of certain truths. I will then

offer an opinion as to how you might most profitably view and respond to those truths.' (I was immediately aware that he didn't seem to be talking about the Advanced Tax final exam.) He said, 'You will return to your homes and families for the holiday vacation and, in that festive interval before the last push of CPA examination study—trust me—you will hesitate, you will feel dread and doubt. This will be natural. You will, for what seems the first time, feel dread at your hometown chums' sallies about accountancy as the career before you, you will read the approval in your parents' smiles as an approval of your surrender—oh, I have been there, gentlemen; I know every cobble in the road you are walking. For the hour approaches. To begin, in that literally dreadful interval of looking down before the leap outward, to hear dolorous forecasts as to the sheer drudgery of the profession you are choosing, the lack of excitement or chance to shine on the athletic fields or ballroom floors of life heretofore.' True, some of it I didn't quite get—I don't think too many of us in the classroom had spent a lot of time 'shining on ballroom floors,' but that might have been just a generational thing—he obviously meant it as a metaphor. I certainly got what he meant about accounting not seeming like a very exciting profession.

The substitute continued, 'To experience commitment as the loss of options, a type of death, the death of childhood's limitless possibility, of the flattery of choice without duress—this will happen, mark me. Childhood's end. The first of many deaths. Hesitation is natural. Doubt is natural.' He smiled slightly. 'You might wish to recall, then, in three weeks' time, should you be so disposed, this room, this moment, and the information I shall now relay to you.'

He was obviously not a very modest or diffident person. On the other hand, his form of address didn't sound nearly as formal or fussy at the time in Advanced Tax as it now sounds when I repeat it—or rather his summation was formal and a bit poetic but not artificially so, like a natural extension of who and what he was. It was not a pose. I remember thinking that maybe the sub had mastered that trick in Uncle Sam posters and certain paintings of seeming to look right at you no matter what angle you faced him from. That perhaps all the hushed and solemn older other students (you could hear a pin) felt picked out and specifically addressed as well—though, of course, that would make no difference as to its special effect on me, which was the real issue, just as the Christian girlfriend's story would have already demonstrated if I'd been aware and attentive enough to hear what the actual point she was trying to make was. As mentioned, the version of me that listened to that story in 1973 or '74 was a nihilistic child.

After one or two other comments, with his hands still clasped behind his back, the substitute continued, 'I wish to inform you that the accounting profession to which you aspire is, in fact, heroic. Please note that I have said "inform" and not "opine" or "allege" or "posit." The truth is that what you soon go home to your carols and toddies and books and CPA examination preparation guides to stand on the cusp of is—heroism.' Obviously, this was dramatic and held everyone's attention. I remember thinking again, as he said this, of the A/V screen's quote I had thought was biblical: 'the moral equivalent of war.' It seemed strange, but not ridiculous. I realized that my thinking about this quote was probably the first time I'd ever considered the word *moral* in any context other than a term paper—this was part of what I had initially started to become aware of a few days prior, in the experience while watching *As the World Turns.* The substitute was only of about average height. His eyes did not cut or wander. Some of the students' glasses reflected light, still. One or two were still taking notes, but other than that, nobody except the substitute spoke or moved.

Continuing on without pause, he said, 'Exacting? Prosaic? Banausic to the point of drudgery? Sometimes. Often tedious? Perhaps. But brave? Worthy? Fitting, sweet? Romantic? Chivalric? Heroic?' When he paused, it wasn't just for effect—at least not totally. 'Gentlemen,' he said, '—by which I mean, of course, latter adolescents who aspire to manhood—gentlemen, here is a truth: Enduring tedium over real time in a confined space is what real courage is. Such endurance is, as it happens, the distillate of what is, today, in this world neither I nor you have made, heroism. Heroism.' He made a point of looking around, gauging people's reaction. Nobody laughed; a few looked puzzled. I remember I was starting to have to go to the bathroom. In the classroom's fluorescent lights, he cast no shadow on any side. 'By which,' he said, 'I mean true heroism, not heroism as you might know it from films or the tales of childhood. You are now nearly at childhood's end; you are ready for the truth's weight, to bear it. The truth is that the heroism of your childhood entertainments was not true valor. It was theater. The grand gesture, the moment of choice, the mortal danger, the external foe, the climactic battle whose outcome resolves all—all designed to appear heroic, to excite and gratify an audience. An audience.' He made a gesture I can't describe: 'Gentlemen, welcome to the world of reality—there is no audience. No one to applaud, to admire. No one to see you. Do you understand? Here is the truth—actual heroism receives no ovation, entertains no one. No one queues up to see it. No one is interested.'

He paused again and smiled in a way that was not one bit self-mocking. 'True heroism is you, alone, in a designated work space. True heroism is minutes, hours, weeks, year upon year of the quiet, precise, judicious exercise of probity and care—with no one there to see or cheer. This is the world. Just you and the job, at your desk. You and the return, you and the cash-flow data, you and the inventory protocol, you and the depreciation schedules, you and the numbers.' His tone was wholly matter-of-fact. It suddenly occurred to me that I had no idea how many words he'd spoken since that 8,206th one at the conclusion of the review. I was aware of how every detail in the classroom appeared very vivid and distinct, as though painstakingly drawn and shaded, and yet also of being completely focused on the substitute Jesuit, who was saying all this very dramatic or even romantic stuff without any of the usual trappings or flourishes of drama, standing now quite still with his hands again behind his back (I knew the hands weren't clasped—I could somehow tell that he was more like holding the right wrist with the left hand) and his face's planes unshadowed in the white light. It felt as though he and I were at opposite ends of some kind of tube or pipe, and that he really was addressing me in particular—although obviously in reality he couldn't have been. The literal reality was that he was addressing me least of all, since obviously I wasn't enrolled in Advanced Tax or getting ready to take the final and then go home and sit at my childhood desk in my old bedroom in my parents' house cramming for the dreaded CPA exam the way it sounded as if many of these others in the room were. Nevertheless—as I wish I'd been able to understand earlier, since it would have saved me a lot of time and cynical drifting—a feeling is a feeling, nor can you argue with results.

Anyhow, meanwhile, in what essentially seemed to be a recapitulation of his main points so far, the substitute said, 'True heroism is *a priori* incompatible with audience or applause or even the bare notice of the common run of man. In fact,' he said, 'the less conventionally heroic or exciting or adverting or even interesting or engaging a labor appears to be, the greater its potential as an arena for actual heroism, and therefore as a denomination of joy unequaled by any you men can yet imagine.' It seemed then that a sudden kind of shudder went through the room, or maybe an ecstatic spasm, communicating itself from senior accounting major or graduate business student to senior accounting major or grad business student so rapidly that the whole collective seemed for an instant to heave—although, again, I am not a hundred percent sure this was real, that it took place outside of me, in the actual classroom, and the (possible) collective spasm's moment was too brief to be more than sort of fleetingly aware of it. I also remember having a strong urge to lean over and tie my boots' laces, which never translated itself into real action.

At the same time, it might be fair to say that I remembered the substitute Jesuit as using pauses and bits of silence rather the way more conventional inspirational speakers use physical gestures and expressions. He said, 'To retain care

and scrupulosity about each detail from within the teeming
wormball of data and rule and exception and contingency
which constitutes real-world accounting—this is heroism.
To attend fully to the interests of the client and to balance
those interests against the high ethical standards of FASB
and extant law—yea, to serve those who care not for service but only for results—this is heroism. This may be
the first time you've heard the truth put plainly, starkly.
Effacement. Sacrifice. Service. To give oneself to the care
of others' money—this is effacement, perdurance, sacrifice, honor, doughtiness, valor. Hear this or not, as you
will. Learn it now, or later—the world has time. Routine,
repetition, tedium, monotony, ephemeracy, inconsequence,
abstraction, disorder, boredom, angst, ennui—these are
the true hero's enemies, and make no mistake, they are
fearsome indeed. For they are real.'

One of the accounting students now raised his hand,
and the substitute paused to answer a question about
adjusted cost basis in the tax classification of gifts. It
was at some point in his answer to this that I heard the
substitute use the phrase 'IRS wiggler.' Since that day, I
have never once heard the term anywhere outside of the
Examination Center at which I'm posted—it is a piece of
Service insider shorthand for a certain class of examiner.
In retrospect, then, this definitely should have raised a
red flag in terms of the substitute's experience and background. (By the way, the term 'FASB' stood for Financial
Accounting Standards Board, though obviously I would
not learn this until entering the Service the following
year.) Also, I should probably acknowledge an obvious
paradox in the memory—despite how attentive and

affected by his remarks about courage and the real world I was, I was not aware that the drama and scintillance I was investing the substitute's words with actually ran counter to those words' whole thrust. That is to say, I was deeply affected and changed by the hortation without, as it now appears, really understanding what he was talking about. In retrospect, this seems like further evidence that I was even more 'lost' and unaware than I knew.

'Too much, you say?' he said. 'Cowboy, paladin, hero? Gentlemen, read your history. Yesterday's hero pushed back at bounds and frontiers—he penetrated, tamed, hewed, shaped, made, brought things into being. Yesterday's society's heroes generated facts. For this is what society is—an agglomeration of facts.' (Obviously, the more real Advanced Tax students who gingerly got up and left, the more my feelings of being particularly, uniquely addressed increased. The older business student with two lush, perfectly trimmed sideburns and incredible notes beside me was able to close his briefcase's metal clasps without any sound at all. On the wire rack beneath his desk was a *Wall Street Journal* that he'd either not read or had perhaps been able to read and refold so perfectly it looked untouched.) 'But it is now today's era, the modern era,' the substitute was saying (which was difficult to argue with, obviously). 'In today's world, boundaries are fixed, and most significant facts have been generated. Gentlemen, the heroic frontier now lies in the ordering and deployment of those facts. Classification, organization, presentation. To put it another way, the pie has been made—the contest is now in the slicing. Gentlemen, you aspire to hold the knife. Wield it. To admeasure. To shape each given slice, the knife's angle and depth of cut.' However transfixed I still was, I was also aware, by this point, that the substitute's metaphors seemed to be getting a bit jumbled—it was hard to imagine the remaining orientals making much sense of cowboys and pies, since they were such specifically American images. He went to the flag-stand in the corner of the room and retrieved his hat, a dark-gray business fedora, old but very well cared for. Instead of putting the hat on, he held it up aloft.

'A baker wears a hat,' he said, 'but it is not our hat. Gentlemen, prepare to wear the hat. You have wondered, perhaps, why all real accountants wear hats? They are today's cowboys. As will you be. Riding the American range. Riding herd on the unending torrent of financial data. The eddies, cataracts, arranged variations, fractious minutiae. You order the data, shepherd it, direct its flow, lead it where it's needed, in the codified form in which it's apposite. You deal in facts, gentlemen, for which there has been a market since man first crept from the primeval slurry. It is you—tell them that. Who ride, man the walls, define the pie, serve.' There was no way not to notice how different he looked now from the way he'd appeared at the beginning. Ultimately, it wasn't clear whether he'd planned or prepared his final hortation or exhortation or not, or whether he was just speaking passionately from the heart. His hat was noticeably more stylish and European-looking than my father's had been, its welt sharper and band's feather pegged—it had to be at least twenty years old. When he raised his arms in conclusion, one hand still held the hat—

'Gentlemen, you are called to account.'

One or two of the remaining students clapped, a some-how terrible sound when it's only a few scattered hands—like a spanking or series of ill-tempered slaps. I remember having a visual flash of something lying in its crib and waving its limbs uselessly in the air, its mouth open and wet. And then of walking back across the transom and down and out of Daniel and over to the library in a strange kind of hyperaware daze, both disoriented and very clear, and then the memory of that incident essentially ends.

After that, the first thing I can remember doing over the holiday recess in Libertyville was getting a haircut. I also then went to Carson Pirie Scott's in Mundelein and bought a dark-gray ventless wool suit with a tight vertical weave and double-pleat trousers, as well as a bulky box-plaid jacket with wide notched lapels, which I ended up almost never wearing, as it had a tendency to roll at the third button and produce what almost looked like a pep-lum when it was buttoned all the way. I also bought a pair of Nunn Bush leather wing tips and three dress shirts—two white oxfords and one light-blue sea island weave. All three collars were of the button-down type.

Except for practically dragging my mother to Wrig-leyville for Christmas dinner at Joyce's, I spent nearly the whole holidays in the house, researching options and requirements. I remember I was also deliberately trying to do some sustained, concentrated thinking. My inner feelings about school and graduating had totally changed. I now felt suddenly and totally behind. It was a bit like the feeling of suddenly looking at your watch and realizing you're late for an appointment, but on a much larger scale. I had only one term left now before I was supposed to graduate, and I was exactly nine required courses short of a major in accounting, to say nothing of trying to sit for the CPA exam. I bought a Barron's guide to the CPA exam at a Waldenbooks in the Galaxy Mall off of Milwaukee Road. It was given three times a year, and it lasted two days, and you were strongly advised to have had both intro and intermediate financial accounting, managerial accounting, two semesters of auditing, business statistics—which, at DePaul, was another famously brutal class—intro data processing, one or preferably two semesters of tax, plus either fiduciary accounting or accounting for nonprofits, and one or more semesters of economics. A fine-print insert also recommended proficiency in at least one 'high-level' computer language like COBOL. The only computer class I'd ever finished was Intro Computer World at UI-Chicago, where we'd mostly played homemade Pong and helped the prof try to recollate 51,000 Hollerith punch cards he'd stored data for a project on and then accidentally dropped on a slick stairway. And so on and so forth. Plus, I looked at a business-stats textbook and discovered that you needed calculus, and I hadn't even had trigonometry—in my senior year of high school, I'd taken Perspectives on Modern Theater instead of trig, which I well remembered my father squeezing my shoes about. Actually, my hatred of Algebra II and refusal to take any more math after that was the occasion for one of the really major arguments that I heard my parents have in the years before they separated, which is all kind of a long story, but I remember overhearing my father saying that there were only two kinds of people in the world—namely, people who actually understood the technical realities of how the real world worked (via, his obvious point was, math and science), and people who didn't—and overhearing my mother being very upset and depressed at what she saw as my father's rigidity and small-mindedness, and her responding that the two basic human types were actually the people so rigid and intolerant that they believed there were only two basic human types, on one side, versus people who believed that there were all different types and varieties of people with their own unique gifts and destinies and paths through life that they had to find, on the other, and so forth. Anyone eavesdropping on the argument, which had started as a typical exchange but escalated into an especially heated one, could quickly tell that the real conflict was between what my mother saw as two extremely different, incompatible ways of seeing the world and treating the people you were supposed to love and support. For instance, it was during this argument that I overheard my father say the thing about my being unable to find my ass even if it had a large bell attached to it, which my mother heard mainly as him passing cold, rigid judgment on somebody he was supposed to love and support, but which, in retrospect, I think might have been the only way my father could find to say that he was worried about me, that I had no initiative or direction, and that he didn't know what to do as a father. As is well-known, parents can have vastly different ways of expressing love and concern. Of course, much of my interpretation is just speculative—there's obviously no way to know what he really meant.

Anyhow, the upshot of all my concentrated thinking and research over the holiday recess was that it looked as though I would basically have to start college all over again, and I was then almost twenty-four. And the financial situation at home was in total flux due to the complex legalities of the wrongful death suit that was under way at the time.

As a side note, there was no amount of alteration that could have made my father's suits fit me. At that time, I was a 40L/30 with a 34 inseam, whereas the bulk of my father's suits were 36R/36/30. The suits and archaic silk blazer ended up being given to Goodwill after Joyce and I cleaned out most of his things from his closet and study and workshop, which was a very sad experience. My mother, as mentioned, was spending more and more time watching the neighborhood birds at the tube feeders which she'd hung around the front porch and the standing feeders in the yard—my father's house's living room had a large picture window with an excellent view of the porch, yard, and street—and often wearing a red chenille robe and large fuzzy slippers all day, and neglecting both her normal interests and personal grooming, which increasingly worried everyone.

After the holidays, just as it was beginning to snow, I made an appointment to speak with DePaul's Associate Dean for Academic Affairs (who was definitely a real Jesuit, and wore the official black-and-white uniform, and also had a yellow ribbon tied to the knob of his office door) about the experience in Advanced Tax and the turnaround in my direction and focus, and about now being so behind in terms of that focus, and to broach the possibility of maybe continuing my enrollment an extra year with deferred tuition in order to help make up some of my deficits in terms of an accounting major. But it was awkward, because I had actually been in this father's office before, two or three years prior, under, to put it mildly, very different circumstances—namely, getting my shoes squeezed and being threatened with academic probation, in response to which I think I may actually have said, aloud, 'Whatever,' which is the sort of thing that Jesuits do not take kindly to. Thus, in this appointment the Associate Dean's demeanor was patronizing and skeptical, and amused—he seemed to find the change in my appearance and stated attitude more comical than anything else, as if he regarded it as a prank or joke, or some kind of ploy to try to buy myself one more year before having to go out and fend for myself in what he termed 'the world of men,' and there was no way to adequately describe for him the awarenesses and conclusions I'd come to while watching daytime television and then later bumbling into the wrong final class without sounding childish or insane, and essentially I was shown the door.

This was in early January 1979, on the day it was just beginning to snow—I can remember watching large, tentative, individual flakes of snow falling and blowing around aimlessly in the wind generated by the train through the window of the CTA commuter line from Lincoln Park back up to Libertyville, and thinking, '*This is my crude approximation of a human life.*' As far as I recall, the yellow ribbons all over the city were because of the hostage trouble in the Mideast and the assault on US embassies. I knew very little about what was going on, partly because I had not watched any TV since that experience in mid-December with the soccer ball and *As the World Turns*. It is not as though I made any conscious decision to renounce television after that time. I just cannot remember watching any after that day. Also, after the pre-holiday experiences, I now felt far too far behind to be able to afford to waste time watching TV. Part of me was frightened that I'd actually become galvanized and motivated too late and was somehow going to just at the last minute 'miss' some crucial chance to renounce nihilism and make a meaningful, real-world choice. This was also all taking place during what emerged as the worst blizzard in the modern history of Chicago, and at the start of the Spring '79 term, everything was in chaos because DePaul's administration kept having to cancel classes because no one who lived off-campus could guarantee they could get in to school, and half of the dorms couldn't reopen yet because of frozen pipes, and part of my father's house's roof cracked because of the weight of accumulated snow and there was a big structural crisis that I got stuck dealing with because my mother was too obsessed with the logistical problems of keeping the snow from covering up all the birdseed she left out. Also, most of the CTA trains were out of service, and buses were abruptly canceled if it was determined that the plows couldn't keep certain roads clear, and every morning of that first week I had to get up very early and listen to the radio to see if DePaul was even having classes that day, and if they were, I'd have to try to slog in. I should mention that my father didn't drive—he'd been a devotee of public transportation—and my mother had given Joyce the Le Car as part of the arrangement they made regarding the dissolution of the bookstore, so there was no car, although occasionally I could get rides from Joyce, although I hated to impose—she was over there mostly to look in on my mother, who was obviously in a decline, and about whom we were all increasingly worried, and it later turned out Joyce had spent a great deal of time doing research into north-county psychological services and programs and trying to determine what kind of special care my mother might need and where it could be found. Despite the snow and temperatures, for instance, my mother now abandoned her practice of watching the birds from inside through the window and progressed to standing on or near the steps to the porch and holding up tube feeders herself in her upraised hands, and appeared prepared to stay in this position long enough to actually develop frostbite if someone didn't intervene and remonstrate with her to come inside. The numbers and noise-level of birds involved were also problematic by this time, as some in the neighborhood had already pointed out even before the blizzard had struck.

On one level, I'm fairly sure that it was on WBBM-AM—a very dry, conservative, all-news station which my father had favored, but whose weather-related cancellations reports were the most comprehensive in the area—that I first heard mention of the Service's aggressive new recruiting-incentive program. 'The Service' obviously being shorthand for the Internal Revenue Service, better known to taxpayers as the IRS. But I also have a partial memory of actually first seeing an advertisement for this recruitment program in a sudden, dramatic way that now, in retrospect, seems so heavily fateful and dramatic that perhaps it is more the memory of a dream or fantasy I had at the time, which essentially consisted of me waiting in the Galaxy Mall food court area while Joyce was helping my mother negotiate another large delivery order from Fish 'n Fowl Pet Plaza. Certain elements of this memory are certainly credible. It is true that I had trouble seeing animals for sale in cages—I have always had difficulty with cages and seeing things caged—and I often did wait for my mother outside in the food court while they were in Fish 'n Fowl. I was there to help carry bags of seed in the event that delivery orders were refused or delayed on account of the severe weather, which, as many Chicagoans still recall, remained intense for quite some time, all but paralyzing the whole area. Anyhow, according to this memory, I was sitting at one of the many stylized plastic tables in the Galaxy Mall's food court, looking absently down at the table's pattern of star- and moon-shaped perforations, and saw, through one such perforation, a portion of the *Sun-Times* that someone had evidently discarded on the floor beneath the table, which was open to the Business Classified section, and the memory involves seeing this from above the table in such a way that a beam of light from the food court's overhead lighting far above fell through one of the star- shaped perforations in the tabletop and illuminated—as if by a symbolically star-shaped spotlight or ray of light—one particular advertisement among all the page's other ads and notices of business and career opportunities, this being a notice about the IRS's new recruitment-incentive program under way in some sections of the country, of which the Chicagoland area was one. I'm simply mentioning this memory, whether it's actually as credible as the more pedestrian WBBM memory or not, as another illustration of how motivationally 'primed' I seemed to be, in retrospect, for a career in the Service.

The IRS recruiting station for the Chicagoland area was in a kind of temporary storefront-type office space on

West Taylor Street, right near to the UIC campus where I'd spent a joyless and hypocritical 1975–76 school year, and almost across the street from the Chicago Fire Department Academy, whose apprentice firemen actually used to show up sometimes in full slicker-and-boot regalia at the Hat, where they were banned from drinks involving seltzer or carbonation of any kind—which involves a long explanation which I won't go into here. Nor, luckily, was the podiatrist's sign with the rotating foot visible from this side of the Kennedy Expressway. That huge, rotating foot represented one of the childish things I was anxious to put away.

I remember the sun had finally emerged—although this later turned out to be only a temporary break or 'eye' in the storm system, and there was more severe winter weather on the way two days hence. There were now four or more feet of new snow on the ground, and much more in places where high-speed plows had cleared the streets and formed mammoth drifts along the sides, and you had to pass through almost a kind of tunnel or nave to get to the sidewalk itself, where you then floundered whenever you passed a property whose owner wasn't civic-minded enough to shovel the sidewalk. I was wearing flared green corduroys whose cuffs were soon almost up around my knees, and my heavy Timberlands—which were not great on actual traction, I had discovered—were packed with snow. It was so bright that it was difficult to see. It felt almost like a polar expedition. When the sidewalks were simply too piled up, you had to try to clamber back over the drifts and walk in the street. Understandably, traffic was light. The streets were now more like canyons with sheer white sides, and the high drifts and business-district buildings beyond cast complex, flat-topped shadows that sometimes formed bar graphs you walked right across. I had been able to catch a bus transfer as far as Grant Park, but no closer. The river was frozen and piled high with snow which the plows had tried to dump there. By the way, I know that it's doubtful that anyone outside the Chicagoland area is very interested in the great 1979 winter storm anymore, but for me it was a vivid, critical time whose memory is unusually clear and focused. To me, this remembered clarity is a further sign of the clear demarcation in my own awareness and sense of direction before and after the substitute in Advanced Tax. It wasn't so much the rhetoric about heroism and wrangling, much of which seemed a bit over-the-top to me even then (there are limits). I think part of what was so galvanizing was the substitute's diagnosis of the world and reality as already essentially penetrated and formed, the real world's constituent info generated, and that now a meaningful choice lay in herding, corralling, and organizing that torrential flow of info. This rang true to me, though on a level that I don't think I even was fully aware existed within me.

Anyhow, it took a while even to find it. I can remember that a few corners' stop signs had only the polygonal sign portion visible above the drifts, and several storefronts' doors had their mail slots frozen open and long tongues of windblown snow on their carpet. Many of the city's maintenance and garbage trucks also had blades affixed to their grilles and were serving as extra plows as Chicago's mayor tried to respond to the public outcry over the inefficient disposal of snow. On Balbo, there were some remains of snowmen in front yards, whose heights indicated the ages of whoever had made them. The storm had blown some of their eyes and pipes away or rearranged their features— from a distance, they looked sinister or deranged. It was very quiet, and so bright that when you closed your eyes there was only a lit-up blood-red in there. There were a few harsh sounds of snow shovels, and a high distant snarling sound that I only later remembered as being one or more snowmobiles on Roosevelt Road. Some of the yards' snowmen wore a father's old or cast-off business hat. One very high, clotted drift had an open umbrella visible at its top, and I recall a frightening few minutes of digging and shouting downward into the hole, because it almost looked as if a person carrying an umbrella might have gotten abruptly buried in mid-stride. But it turned out to be just an umbrella which someone had abandoned by opening it and shoving it handle-down into the snowbank, perhaps as some kind of prank or gesture to play with people's minds.

Anyhow, it emerged that the Service had recently instituted a program of recruiting new contract employees in much the same way as the new volunteer armed forces— with heavy advertising and inducements. There turned out to be good institutional reasons for the aggressive recruiting, only some of which had to do with competition from the private accounting sector.

By the way, only lay and popular media refer to all IRS contract employees as 'agents.' Within the Service, where personnel are more often identified by the branch or division in which they're posted, 'agent' usually refers to those in the Criminal Investigation Division, which is comparatively small and handles cases of tax evasion so egregious that criminal penalties more or less have to be sought in order to make an example of the TP, which is essentially designed to motivate overall compliance. (By the way, given that the federal tax system still proceeds largely on voluntary compliance, the psychology of the Service's relation to taxpayers is complex, requiring a public impression of extreme efficiency and thoroughness, together with an aggressive system of penalties, interest, and, in extreme cases, criminal prosecution. In reality, though, Criminal Investigations is somewhat of a last resort, since criminal penalties rarely tend to yield additional revenue—a TP in prison has no income and is thus obviously not in a position to pay down his delinquency—whereas the credible threat of prosecution can function as a spur to repayment and future compliance, as well as having a motivating effect on other taxpayers considering criminal evasions. For the Service, in other words, 'public relations' is actually a vital, complex part of both mission and efficacy.) Similarly, while 'examiner' is often the popular term—even among some private tax professionals—for the IRS employee who conducts an audit, whether in the field or the appropriate District office, the Service's own internal term for such a post is 'auditor'—the term 'examiner' refers to an employee tasked with the actual selection of certain tax returns for audit, although he never deals with the TP directly. Examinations is, as mentioned, the responsibility of Regional Examination Centers such as Peoria's Midwest REC. Organizationally, Examinations, Audits, and Criminal Investigation are all divisions of the IRS's Compliance Branch. At the same time, though, it is true that certain mid-level auditors are known technically within the Service's personnel

hierarchy as 'revenue agents.' It's also true that members of
the Internal Inspections Division are sometimes classified
as 'agents,' with the Inspections Division being rather like
the Service's version of law enforcement agencies' Internal Affairs. In essence, they are tasked with investigating
charges of malfeasance or criminal behavior on the part of
Service employees or administration. Administratively, IID
is part of the Internal Control Branch of the IRS, which
also includes both the Personnel and Systems Divisions.
The point, I suppose, is that, as with most large federal
agencies, the structure and organization of the Service is
highly complex—in fact, there are departments within the
Internal Control branch tasked exclusively to studying the
Service's own organizational structure and determining
ways to help maximize efficiency in terms of the Service's
mission.

Set amid the dazzling paralysis of the Chicago Loop,
the IRS recruiting station was not, at first blush, a very
dramatic or compelling-looking place. There was also a US
Air Force recruiting office in the same storefront, separated
from the IRS's space only by a large polyvinyl screen or
shield, and the fact that the USAF office played an orches-
tral version of the familiar 'Off we go into the wild blue
yonder' musical theme over and over again on a repeating
track in its reception area may well have had something
to do with the IRS recruiter's problem with his head and
face, which were prone to small spastic jerks and grimaces
at various times, and was, at first, difficult not to stare at
and to act casual in the presence of. This Service recruiter,
who appeared unshaven and had a cowlick that seemed to
comprise almost the whole right side of his head, also wore

his sunglasses indoors, and had an involved stain on one lapel of his suit jacket, and his necktie—unless my eyes had not yet adjusted from the brilliant dazzle of floundering southwest through fallen snow all the way from the Buckingham Fountain bus stop in Grant Park—might have been an actual clip-on. On the other hand, I had melted snow up to my groin, and frozen birdseed on my down coat, as well as two different winter-weight turtlenecks on beneath that, and probably did not look very promising either. (There was obviously no way that I was going to wear any of my new Carson's business apparel to clamber through chest-high snowdrifts.) Besides the distracting martial music from across the screen, the IRS recruiting station itself was overheated, and smelled of sour coffee and a brand of stick-style deodorant which I couldn't place. Several empty Nesbitt's soda cans were arranged atop an overfull wastebasket, around which a litter of balled-up papers suggested idle hours of trying to throw balled-up papers into it—a pastime I knew well from 'studying' at the UIC library on the evenings when the podiatrist's sign's foot had so ruled. I also remember an open box of doughnuts whose glaze had gone unappetizingly dull.

Nevertheless, I wasn't here to judge anything, nor to make hasty commitments. I was here to try to verify the seemingly almost incredible incentives for entering the Service that had been detailed by the advertisement I'd either heard or perhaps seen two days prior. It eventually emerged that the recruiter had been on duty without relief for several days because of the storm, which was probably the reason for his condition—the Service's standards for personal appearance on-post are normally fairly stringent.

When one of the city's large, makeshift plows came by, the noise shook the storefront's window, which faced south and was untinted—forming another possible explanation for the recruiter's sunglasses, which I still found disconcerting. The recruiter's desk was flanked by flags and a large easel with institutional charts and advertisements on large pieces of posterboard, and hanging slightly askew on the wall above and behind the desk was a framed print of the Internal Revenue Service seal, which, the recruiter explained, depicted the mythic hero Bellerophon slaying the Chimera, as well as the Latin motto on a long furling banner along the bottom, *'Alicui tamen faciendum est,'* which essentially means *'He is the one doing a difficult, unpopular job.'* It turned out that, for reasons dating all the way back to the permanent institution of a federal income tax in 1913, Bellerophon was the Service's official symbol or figure, rather the way the bald eagle is the United States as a whole's.

In return for a commitment of two to four years, depending on the specific incentive scheme, the Internal Revenue Service was offering up to a total of $14,450 for college or continuing technical education. That was, of course, $14,450 before applicable taxes, I remember the IRS recruiter stipulating with a smile I did not, at that point, know how to interpret. Also, by an elaborate arrangement which the recruiter highlighted for me on a fold-out document that outlined all the Service's various incentive schedules in complex diagrams with dotted lines and extremely small type, if the continuing education led to either a CPA license or a master's degree in the accounting or tax fields from an accredited institution, there were several grades of further inducements to extend one's employee contract with the IRS, including an option to attend classes while posted at either a Regional Service Center or Regional Examination Center, to which the recruiter explained that newer Service personnel were commonly posted for their first several quarters after what the recruiter called 'T and A.' In order to qualify for the incentive package, one had to complete the twelve-week course at an IRS Training and Assessment Center, or TAC, which is what the recruiter's rather cynical 'T and A' also stood for. Also, employees nearly always refer to the IRS as 'the Service,' and the site at which one works as their IRS 'Post,' and they measure time of employment not in years or months but in terms of the Service calendar's four fiscal quarters, which correspond to the legal deadlines for mailing quarterly estimated tax, or 1040-EST, payments, the only unusual thing about which is that the second quarter runs from 15 April to 15 June, or only two months, and the fourth extends from 15 September to 15 January of the successive year—this is mainly so that the final quarter can comprise the entire taxable year through 31 December. The recruiter explained none of this in so many words at the time—much of it is just the sort of special institutional info one absorbs over time in an adult career.

Anyhow, by this time there were also two other would-be recruits in the office, one of whom I only remember as having a brightly colored one-piece snowsuit and a somewhat low, bulging forehead. The other, older man, though, had masking or duct tape holding his battered sneakers' soles on, and was shivering in a way that seemed to have nothing to do with temperature, and impressed me as quite probably an indigent or street person rather than

a bona fide candidate for recruitment. I was trying to concentrate and study the incentive-schedule handout in my
hand throughout the recruiter's more formal introductory
presentation, and as a result, I know I failed to catch certain key details. Also, though, those details were sometimes
actually drowned out by the cymbals and timpanis of the
Air Force theme's crescendo portion on the screen's other
side. We three, the recruiting presentation's audience, were
in folding metal chairs arranged before his desk, which the
recruiter initially stood to the side of, beside his display
easel—I remember that the man with the low forehead had
reversed his chair and was seated leaning forward with his
hands on the chair's back and his chin atop his knuckles,
whereas the third member of our audience was eating a
doughnut after placing several others in side pockets of his
khaki army coat. I remember the Service recruiter contin-
ually referred to an elaborate color chart or diagram that
depicted the administrative structure and organization of
the IRS. The depiction covered more than one chart, actually, and the recruiter—who sneezed several times without
covering his nose or even averting his head, and also had
more of the tiny neurological tic- or spasm-events at certain
points in the unavoidably overheard 'Off we go . . .'—had
to keep pulling different sections of posterboard to the
front of the easel, and the whole thing was so complicated, and consisted of so many branches, sub-branches,
divisions, and coordinating offices and sub-offices, as well
as parallel or bilateral sub-offices and technology support
divisions, that it appeared impossible to comprehend even
the general sense of well enough to take a real interest in,
though I obviously made it a conscious point to look as

attentive and engaged as possible, if only to show that I was someone who could be trained to herd and process large amounts of info. At that juncture, I was obviously unaware that initial diagnostic screening of possible recruits was already under way, and that the excessive complexity and minutiae of the recruiter's presentation represented part of a psychological 'dispositional assessment' mechanism in use by the IRS's Personnel Division since 1967. Nor did I understand, when the other potential recruit (meaning the one who wasn't obviously just looking for a warm place off the street) began nodding off over his chair's back at the abstruseness of the presentation, that he had effectively eliminated himself as a candidate for all but the lowest-level IRS postings. Also, there were upwards of twenty different forms to fill out, many of which were redundant—it wasn't clear to me why one couldn't simply fill out one copy and then xerox a number of duplicates, but I again chose to keep my own counsel and simply fill out the same essential info over and over again.

Overall, despite comprising scarcely more than 5,750 total words, the initial recruiting presentation and processing lasted almost three hours, during which there were also several intervals when the recruiter trailed off and sat in a heavy, incongruous silence during which he may or may not have been asleep—the sunglasses made it impossible to verify. (I would later be informed that these unexplained pauses, too, were part of initial recruit screening and 'dispositional assessment,' that the shabby recruiting office was, in fact, under sophisticated videotape surveillance—one of the required forms had contained an 'Authorization to Record' buried in one of the subclause's boilerplate,

which I obviously did not notice at the time—and that
our fidget- and yawn-rates and certain characteristics of
posture, position, and facial expression in certain contexts
would be reviewed and compared to various psychological templates and predictive formulas which the Service's
Internal Control Branch's Personnel Division's Recruitment and Training subdivision had developed several years
prior, which is, in turn, a very long and complicated story
involving the Service's emphasis, throughout the 1960s and
'70s, on maximizing 'throughput,' meaning the highest
possible efficiency in terms of the volume of tax returns and
documents that could be processed, examined, audited,
and adjusted in a given fiscal quarter. Though the Service's
concept of efficiency would undergo changes in the 1980s,
as new government priorities trickled down through the
Treasury and Triple-Six, with an institutional emphasis on
maximizing revenue rather than throughput of returns, the
emphasis at the time—meaning January 1979—required
screening recruits for a set of characteristics that boiled
down to an ability to maintain concentration under con-
ditions of extreme tedium, complication, confusion, and
absence of comprehensive info. The Service was, in the
words of one of the Examinations instructors at the Indianapolis TAC, looking for 'cogs, not spark plugs.'

Eventually, it was beginning to get dark and to snow
again by the time the recruiter announced that the process
was over, and we—by this time there were perhaps five or
six of us in the audience, some having drifted in during the
formal presentation—were then each given a ream-sized
stack of stapled packets of materials in a large blue IRS
binder. The recruiter's final instructions were that those

of us who felt we were still potentially interested should go home and read these materials closely, and return the next day—which would, if I remember right, have been a Friday—for the next stage of the recruitment process.

To be honest, I had expected to be interviewed and asked all sorts of questions about my background, experience, and direction in terms of career and commitment. I expected that they would want to verify I was serious and not just there to scam the IRS out of free tuition funding. Not surprisingly, I had expected that the Internal Revenue Service—which my father, whose job with the city had understandably involved dealings with the IRS on a variety of levels, feared and respected—would be acutely sensitive to the possibility of being scammed or conned in any way, and I remember, on the long trek in from the bus stop, that I had been apprehensive about what to say in response to tough questioning about the origin of my interest and goals. I'd been concerned about how to tell the truth without the Service's recruiters reacting the way the Associate Dean for Academic Affairs had just recently reacted, or thinking of me in anything like the way I had thought about the Christian girl with the multifloral boots in the Lindenhurst memory already mentioned. To the best of my recollection, though, I was required to say almost nothing that first day of recruiting after the initial hello and one or two innocuous questions—as well as my name, of course. Nearly all my input was, as I've mentioned, in the form of forms, many of which had bar codes in the lower left corners—this detail I remember because these were the first bar codes I can remember ever being aware of in my life up to then.

Anyhow, the recruiting office's binder full of homework was so unbelievably dry and obscure that you essentially had to read each line several times to derive any sense of what it was trying to say. I almost couldn't believe it. I had already gotten a taste of real accounting language from the assigned textbooks for Managerial Accounting and Auditing I, which were both just under way—when weather permitted—at DePaul, but the Service material made those textbooks look like child's play by comparison. The largest single packet in the binder was something on low-toner Xerox called *Statement of Procedural Rules,* which is actually from Title 26, §601 of the *Code of Federal Regulations.* A ninety-five-word section of a page that I remember that I flipped to at first at random and read, just to get an idea of what I would be having to try to read and process, was ¶1910, §601.201a(1)(g), subpart xi:

> For ruling requests concerning the classification of an organization as a limited partnership where a corporation is the sole general partner, see Rev. Proc. 72–13, 1972–1 CB 735. See also Rev. Proc. 74–17, 1974–1 CB 438, and Rev. Proc. 75–16, 1975–1 CB 676. Revenue Procedure 74–17 announces certain operating rules of the Service relating to the issuance of advance ruling letters concerning the classification of organizations formed as limited partnerships. Revenue Procedure 75–16 sets forth a checklist outlining required information frequently omitted from requests for rulings relating to classification of organizations for Federal tax purposes.

Essentially, the whole thing was like that. Nor, at the time, did I know we would have to try to practically memorize the entire 82,617-word *Procedural Rules* manual at the Training and Assessment Center, less for informational purposes—since every IRS examiner's Tingle table would have the *Procedural Rules* included in the *Internal Revenue Manual* right there in the bottom-right drawer, attached with a little chain so no one could take or borrow it, as we were all supposed to have it at our Tingle at all times—but more as a type of diagnostic tool for seeing who could sit there hour after hour and apply themselves to it versus who couldn't, which obviously bore on who could cut it at various levels of complexity and dryness (which, in turn, is why the Examinations component of the TAC's training course was known at the TAC as 'Camp Concentration'). My best guess at the time, sitting there in my childhood room in my father's house in Libertyville (the dorm at DePaul still wasn't open, as some frozen pipes had ruptured—the storm and its fallout still had much of the city paralyzed), was that requiring us to read this material was some kind of test or hurdle to help determine who was truly motivated and serious and who was just drifting around attempting to scam some easy tuition money from the government. I kept picturing the indigent character who ate all the doughnuts from that afternoon's presentation lying in a cardboard appliance box in an alley, reading a page of the packet and then setting it afire to provide light for reading the next page. In a certain way, I think that that was essentially what I was doing, too—I had to blow off nearly all my next day's accounting class assignments in order to stay up nearly all night getting through the Service material.

It didn't feel feckless, though it also didn't feel especially romantic or heroic. It was more as if I simply had to make a choice of what was more important.

I read more or less the whole thing. I won't even say how many words in toto. It took until almost 5:00 A.M. At the very back—not all the way, but tucked between two pages of the transcript of a 1966 USTC case called *Uinta Livestock Corporation v. U.S.* near the back of the binder—were a couple of more forms to fill out, which reinforced my assumption that it really had been a kind of test to see if we were committed and interested enough to nut up and plow all the way through. I can't say I read everything carefully, of course. One of the few packets that wasn't totally eye-glazing was a rundown on the IRS Training and Assessment Centers and on the various types of entry-level posts available to recruits who came out of the TAC course with various levels of education and incentive packages. There were two IRS Training and Assessment Centers, in Indianapolis and Columbus, OH, about which the packet had photos and regulations but nothing specific on what the training was actually like. As usually happens with photocopied photos, the images were mostly black masses with some indistinct white blobs; you couldn't really make out what was going on. Unlike the present day, the protocol in that era was that if you wanted a serious career in the Service, with a contract and civil service rank above GS-9, you had to go through a TAC course, which lasted twelve weeks. You also had to join the Treasury Employees union, although info on that criterion was not included in the packet. Otherwise you were, in essence, a temporary or seasonal worker, which the

Service uses a lot of, especially in the lower levels of Returns Processing and Exams. I remember that the Post List's representation of the Service's structure was much simpler and less comprehensive than the recruiter's presentation's diagram, although this one also had a lot of asterisks and single and double lines connecting various parts of the page's grid, and the legend for these marks had been half cut off due to someone having xeroxed the thing at an angle. In that era, the six main nodes or Service branches consisted of Administration, Returns Processing, Compliance, Collections, Internal Control, Support Services, and something called Technical Branch, which was the only branch with the actual word *Branch* in its name on the diagram, which at the time I found curious. Each branch then branched into several subordinate divisions—thirty-six divisions in all, though in today's Service there are now forty-eight separate divisions, some with cross-coordinated and overlapping functions which have to be streamlined and overseen by the Divisional Liaison Division, which is itself—somewhat confusingly—a division of both the Administration and Internal Control Branches. Each division then also comprised numerous subdivisions, some of whose typeface got extremely small and hard to read. The Compliance Branch's Examinations Division, for example, comprised positions—though only those postings marked in italic font (which was practically impossible to make out on the Xerox) required a federal contract or TAC course— in clerical, cart, data entry, data processing, classification, correspondence, district office interface, regional office interface, duplicating services, procurement, research audit interface, secretarial, personnel, service center interface, computer center interface, and so forth, as well as formal 'rote examiner' posts grouped (in that era, though here at the Midwest REC now the group characterizations are quite a bit different) by the types of returns one specialized in, encoded on the diagram as 1040, 1040A, 1041, EST, and 'Fats,' which refers to a complex 1040 with more than four schedules or attachments. Also, corporate 1120 and 1120S tax returns are examined by special examiners known in Exams as 'immersives,' which the recruiting page did not include information on, as immersive exams are conducted by special elite, highly trained examiners who have their own special section of the REC facility.

Anyhow, as I still can recall, the obvious idea was that anyone who was truly serious would make their best attempt to read the whole contents of the binder, would see and complete the relevant portions of the forms at the back, and then would make the effort to somehow commute back in, weather permitting, to the West Taylor recruiting station the next day by 9:00 A.M. for something which the final sheet termed 'advanced processing.' It also snowed all night again, though not as heavily, and by 4:00 A.M. you could hear the terrible sound of the City of Libertyville's plows scraping the street's concrete raw outside my childhood room's window—also, the bird-sounds at sunrise were incredible, causing lights in some of the other houses along our street to come on in irritation—and the CTA was still only running a staggered schedule. Still, even given the rush of commuters at that time of day and the rigors of the trek in from Grant Park, I arrived back at the storefront recruiting station no later than 9:20 A.M. (albeit covered with snow again), to find no one else there from the prior day except the same Service recruiter, looking even more exhausted and disheveled, who, when I came in and said I was ready for advanced processing, and gave him the forms from the homework I'd plowed through, looked from me to the forms and back again, giving me the exact kind of smile of someone who, on Christmas morning, has just unwrapped an expensive present he already owns.

McNally Editions reissues books that are not widely known but have stood the test of time, that remain as singular and engaging as when they were written. Available in the US wherever books are sold or by subscription from mcnallyeditions.com.